DAYS OF SUMMER

A NOVEL

MELISSA HILL

Originally published in the US as
'Summer at the Heartbreak Cafe'
Copyright © Melissa Hill 2023

The right of Melissa Hill to be identified as the Author of the Work has been asserted by her in accordance with the Copyright, Designs and Patents Act 1988.

All rights reserved. No part of this publication may be reproduced, stored in a retrieval system, or transmitted, in any form or by any means without the prior written permission of the author. You must not circulate this book in any format.

All characters in this publication are fictitious and any resemblance to real persons, living or dead is purely coincidental.

1

Like a wheel of fortune that had last stopped in the depths of winter, the weather had since spun again and laid to rest at where summer sunshine bathed the Irish countryside.

Ella Harris looked up at the clear blue skies and smiled.

It was early June, and today the sun had some real warmth to it for the first time. With days of summer came a lifting of the spirits and a feeling of general optimism.

In her sixty-odd years she had learned to appreciate all seasons, but summer was without doubt her favourite time of the year.

"Isn't it glorious?" she said to Nina, her friend and

part-time waitress in the cafe Ella ran in Lakeview, a beloved Irish tourist destination.

Twenty minutes-drive from Dublin City, the town was centred round a broad oxbow lake from which it took its name.

The lake, surrounded by low-hanging beech and willow trees, wound its way around the centre and a small humpback stone bridge joined all sides of the township together.

The cobbled streets and ornate lanterns on Main Street, plus the beautiful one-hundred-year-old artisan cottages decorated with hanging floral baskets, had resulted in heritage status designation by the Irish Tourist Board, and the chocolate-box look and feel was intentionally well preserved.

Ella's café was situated in a small two-storey building with an enviable position right at the edge of the lake and on the corner where Main Street began.

Early in their marriage, she and her husband Gregory took over the running of the café from her father-in-law, and Ella had spent nearly every waking moment since then ensuring that his legacy—and that of her dearly departed husband—lived on through good food, hot coffee and warm conversation.

"Bliss," Nina agreed wistfully. "I adore summer. No more school runs and trying to rush little Patrick out the door in the mornings,' she said fondly, referring to her five year old son.

Ella smiled, thinking not for the first time that the younger woman was doing a wonderful job of bringing up her little boy alone.

Though she knew Nina had some help from her father - after whom her son was named - being a single mum in a small Irish community wasn't an easy prospect, and she was glad that Nina had overcome her initial indecision about whether Lakeview was the best place to be, as opposed to the city where her mother resided.

Ella was also glad that a few hours a day working at the cafe at busier times helped provide a little extra income for Nina, as well as the opportunity to get out and about. Summer was one of those times.

For Ella, there was no question that Lakeview was the best place to be, but that was easy for her to say. She'd enjoyed a very happy life here, raised three wonderful children with Gregory and despite burying her husband almost a decade ago had even recently managed to find love again.

She smiled as she thought of the new man in her life - fellow Lakeview native Joseph - and what a whirlwind the last six months had been.

Now, the two women systematically opened each

of the ten parasols providing shade for the outdoor seating area overlooking the park by the lake.

Set up for the summer season, the terrace boasted comfortable bistro chairs and tables, plus pretty red and white striped parasols. The cafe's al fresco dining area was now well and truly ready for summer and the town's habitual influx of tourists.

Ella picked up her cleaning bucket and put it next to Nina's before returning inside the cafe through the side door.

As always, the interior felt immediately warm and inviting, with delicious scents emanating from the kitchen.

She stopped to survey the space. The decor hadn't changed much over the years — it was still a warm cosy room with parquet oak flooring, shelves full of dried flowers and old country-style knick-knacks, along with haphazard seating and mismatched tables, one of which was an antique Singer sewing table.

In front of the kitchen and serving area was a long granite countertop, where any solo customers typically nursed coffees and pastries atop a row of stools.

Alongside this was a glass display case filled with a selection of freshly baked goods; muffins, doughnuts, carrot cake, brownies and cream puffs for the sweet-toothed, as well as pies, sausage rolls and Italian breads for the more savoury-orientated.

From early morning the cafe was flooded with families, friends and neighbours, all there to grab a bite to eat—and to gossip.

Ella thrived on the buzz and commotion, and the community embraced her in turn: she had become a bit of a town figurehead and confidant to anyone who came in looking for some conversation with their coffee.

The walls were adorned with watercolours by popular Dublin artist Myra Smith, who routinely spent the days of summer in town working on her paintings, staying at one of the nearby artisan cottages - many of which were rented out to holidaymakers at this time of year.

The artist had donated a couple of paintings to the cafe as a thank you a couple of years before, and now even though she was widely famous and sought-after, Myra still popped in now and again.

This room was heavy with memories and all the people whose lives had merged there and Ella reached under her spectacles and dabbed at her eyes.

Why was she so emotional this morning?

Then she remembered that this always happened at the start of summer, before the small community swelled with visitors from near and far, changing the dynamic of both the town and the cafe.

Like every other gone by, Ella hoped that this year's days of summer would be good for Lakeview, and she looked forward to welcoming new visitors whose arrival always managed to create some drama.

2

"You look so thoughtful," Colm, the cafe's resident chef called out from behind the counter. He was a true gem and had been working for Ella since he was still in school.

She was the first person he'd come out to - a difficult prospect for someone in a small Irish community like this - and they were great friends.

Colm lived with his partner in one of the artisan cottages nearby, but the two men spent a lot of time travelling the world, jetting off at quieter times of the year, during which time Ella held the fort herself.

She chuckled. "Just indulging in past memories. The Heartbreak Cafe has seen its fair share of drama," she joked, referring to the cafe's popular nickname.

Colm rolled his eyes.

"Well, if the last thirty years have been like the last two or three, it must have been crazy altogether," he said, referring to recent personal and community dramas that were somehow always central to this place.

Ella walked a few steps to the front of the counter. The glass surrounding it was sparkling clean; as always Nina had done a wonderful job.

Going out front, she looked up and down along Main Street. Already there was a hustle and bustle that had been absent over the last few months in the lull between Christmas and early summer.

She saw Paddy Collins walking slowly down the street, his walking stick tapping the ground in front of him.

"Hello Paddy," Ella greeted with a smile. "Time to get out of hibernation?"

He chuckled, the wrinkles around his mouth creasing even deeper. "You're right there. Any chance of a warm cuppa for an ould man, and maybe an omelette while you're at it?"

"Of course. Come on in."

Ella led the way and duly went behind the counter.

"Cheese and tomato omelette please Colm, our first official customer of the summer is here."

"Our resident swallow?"

Ella nodded. "Yep, it is indeed Paddy."

"Then summer has now *officially* begun," the chef declared and retreated to the kitchen.

It was true, Ella thought as a few minutes later, she arranged the food on a tray, Paddy was as regular as the seasons themselves.

When autumn arrived, he retreated into his cottage and rarely ventured out. He had a daughter, Elizabeth who stayed and kept him company during the harsher winter months.

But every year without fail, when the weather changed, almost like a squirrel which had been resting underground, Paddy Collins left his cottage and ventured out, and his first stop was always her cafe.

For the next few months, Ella knew he would eat breakfast at her establishment every single morning and she was only too delighted to have him.

"Is Elizabeth all right?" she asked, placing the tray in front of Paddy. He had chosen the same table he always did, next to the front widow where he could watched people passing by on the street outside.

"Oh she's grand, gone up north for a while," he told her.

"Shame that she doesn't spend summer here with us too," Ella commented.

"Ah, I've tried to talk to her but she'll hear nothing of it. Says this place holds too many memories," Paddy said, cutting up his omelette in a painstakingly slow way.

Ella knew why his daughter avoided being in Lakeview at this time of year.

One summer very many years ago, a handsome tourist had come into town and he and Elizabeth had fallen deeply in love. The young couple had spent the summer together, and when it was over, the tourist proposed and they went on to make plans for their future.

The wedding was planned for the following spring, and it was to be the wedding of the year.

Elizabeth's new fiancé returned to Dublin, supposedly to sort out his affairs, but never returned. Paddy's daughter was crushed. She had never truly moved on from that experience, viewing all men as the enemy.

"Maybe one day, she'll find someone else, and get over all that," Ella mused.

"Sure there's nothing I or anybody else can do for her," Paddy muttered, evidently eager to get on with his breakfast.

After that, the café got busy with regulars coming in for breakfast, or midmorning coffee.

Around midday, when there was a typical lull in

activity before the lunchtime crowd, a handsome stranger walked in, standing uncertainly in the middle of the room as he scanned the bakery counter.

And here we go, Ella noted smiling, *our first summer visitor.*

3

Sam Crosby looked approvingly around the little town that was to be his summer retreat.

Coming to Lakeview had been a brainwave. Already he could feel his muscles relaxing and the tension from the last couple of weeks ebbing away.

His hands were tucked inside the front pockets of his jeans as he contemplated his new surroundings. Hopefully he would leave this place with a first draft of the new novel.

If not, he had no idea what to do.

It wasn't writer's block; Sam didn't believe in all that malarkey; it was simply a lack of a good plot.

He'd discarded all the story ideas that came to his

mind so far. They were nonsense and lacked the meat to carry a novel to the end.

He slowed his step to take in the tantalising scent of fresh bread. A little way down was a café, the Heartbreak Cafe he'd heard his landlady call it, and the enticing cooking smells reminded Sam that he had not eaten since breakfast.

He had arrived in the town half an hour ago, and hadn't even unpacked his things in the pretty cottage he was staying at. His agent had found him the quaint little place by the lake, and if the easygoing surroundings didn't get his creative juices flowing, nothing else would.

The holiday cottages were also just a short walk from Main Street.

Now, he went into the café and behind the counter was a dignified older lady with more grey hair than black, and a younger waitress. She was very pretty, with flowing dark hair parted in the middle and pale eyes that fell between blue and grey.

"Hello and welcome," the older woman greeted, smiling at Sam as if they were long lost friends. "You must be one of our summer visitors."

He looked at her, a little at a loss to what response was appropriate.

So much for peace and quiet. "I guess I am."

"Please, take a table anywhere and we'll be right with you."

He chose a table by the window, next to an old man sipping his tea. The man focused his grey watery eyes on Sam for a few seconds and then looked away disinterested.

Sam looked around. Ella was friendly and warm as she took his order, and immediately made him feel right at home. He felt a little ashamed of himself for his initial gruffness towards her.

But the last thing he wanted right now was chatty locals distracting him.

What he needed for his creativity to emerge was focus.

He hadn't come to Lakeview to make friends. Sam was here to finish his novel and was determined to do just that.

By the end of the summer, his publisher expected something from him, and Sam knew he needed to deliver. Readers too were waiting on something new.

In this day and age, if he didn't come up with something great his name and reputation would be quickly forgotten.

Why now? He had never run out of ideas before.

Sam suspected that it had something to do with working nonstop over the years. Each year for the last three years, he'd had two novels published, all six of which had been bestsellers.

It was a lot of pressure, so much expectation.

You never knew with books. His favourite was *The End of Time*, which he had written five years ago.

It had gone dismally; in fact, it was his poorest performing publication ever. Yet even today, Sam still considered it the best thing he had ever written.

Typical.

The older lady returned to his table with a tray bearing his coffee and a doorstep of a sandwich.

"Are you staying in the holiday cottages by the lake?" Ella enquired.

"Yes," Sam nodded with a smile, trying to sound a bit more friendly. "It's a great spot, and this is a lovely town."

"Glad you think so. How long are you staying?"

"A couple of months,' he replied.

Her eyebrows curved. "Oh, so you're the author then?"

"Yes, that's me," he confirmed in a flat voice.

He liked his privacy and hated the fact that this Ella already seemed to know about him.

Experience had taught him to keep his occupation to himself. There were would-be writers everywhere, and while he was happy to give pointers and talks at organised events, it was distracting to be bombarded by people asking about his books and whether or not they'd 'heard of him.'

"Don't worry; no one will bother you here," Ella continued, as if reading his thoughts. "We love visitors, but we also know how to give them their privacy. You'll work in peace here," she added with a reassuring smile.

"I very much hope so," Sam said, aware he was being curt again, but unable to help it due to the tension in his body.

Ella took the hint and with one last smile, she padded away.

Sam chewed on his sandwich, as he looked out the window and took in the passers-by outside on Main Street.

Peace, in a buzzy place like this?

Now, he wasn't so sure.

4

"Have you packed the boys' swimming costumes?" Grace Carter asked, speaking in hushed tones.

Her four year old twin sons were asleep for their afternoon nap, and that hour of silence was precious.

"Yes, everything is ready," Marie their long-time nanny said.

Grace looked at her with a sad smile. "I so wish you were coming with us."

"Me too Mrs Carter, but it's a good opportunity for me to go and see my mother."

Marie was from Colombia and had worked for the Carters ever since the birth of twins, Josh and Jake.

She was capable and motherly and handled the boys in a way Grace herself had never seemed able to.

She would miss Marie for the time she would be away, but the family was also looking forward to their own holiday and some time away from the hustle and bustle of city life.

The sound of a car in the driveway broke into Grace's thoughts and she went downstairs.

"You're early today," she said to her husband.

"Yes, I wanted to surprise you," Kevin said, dropping his laptop on the small table by the hallway and loosening his tie.

Grace tilted her head and smiled fondly. Kevin looked perpetually harassed. His short hair - dirty blond and curly - was untidy from constantly running his hand through it. His tie hung askew on the left side and his eyes looked tired.

"You look like you could do with a rest."

"Yes, but that's not going to happen," he said tersely. "Let's go into the living room for a second, OK?"

Grace's insides twisted immediately at the realisation that something was wrong.

Had Kevin lost his job?

Her heart beat fast, knowing what a disaster that would be. They had a huge mortgage and she was just thinking of returning to university for her master's degree and then get a job, after four years of being an (admittedly part-time) stay-at-home-mum.

Oh no, please don't let it be that he has lost his job.

Grace clenched and unclenched her hands as she followed her husband into the living room. She sat on the edge of the chair facing Kevin, the coffee table between them.

Her brain which had been swarming with jumbled up thoughts was now still, as she braced herself to hear his news.

"It's about this trip…" Kevin began.

Her body relaxed a little. Maybe he hadn't lost his job after all.

"I can't go, honey, not now. Back in January when we booked it, all seemed fine but there's just too much going on at the moment with the takeover. I can't just take a big chunk of time off. Not now at least. I can maybe try and go down there at weekends though?"

Grace's first reaction was relief. Relief that normal family existence could continue uninterrupted. It didn't last long though. Her mind shifted quickly to the upcoming summer holiday to Wicklow, and her eyes widened.

"So I'll be going alone with the boys?" She wasn't sure if this notion was more terrifying than the idea of Kevin losing his job.

"You'll be fine. In fact you'll be better off without me. You get to do what you want whenever you want, without three men in the mix."

"No. Let's cancel the trip altogether," Grace said, a panicky feeling crawling from her toes so that by the time it got to her chest, she felt incapable of thought.

"What? Why? Of course you'll be fine. Besides, the boys are so excited about going to the lake."

"But what if something goes wrong while we're there?"

"Like what?"

"What if they get sick?"

"There are GPs in Lakeview," Kevin pointed out.

Grace tried to think of the million other things that could go wrong with her taking care of the twins on her own in a strange place for so long.

Kevin sounded so confident in her abilities, yet that heavy feeling in her stomach refused to go away.

In theory, going to the small holiday town with her twin sons over the summer didn't sound so difficult, but in practice, it was a whole different ball game.

Grace found herself nodding and agreeing although she didn't have much of a choice really.

As an executive of one of the top marketing firms in the country, which had just been taken over by the biggest, Kevin's job was a big deal, and they couldn't jeopardise that.

5

The shrill of the landline broke the silence in the house. Grace stood up quickly and went to the hallway hoping the noise had not woken up the twins.

"Hello," she greeted into the receiver.

"Hi Grace, its Christine. I was just calling to remind you about those summer classes for the boys? I've signed my two up for Life Skills next week and Taekwondo after that. There's also piano lessons at the -"

Once again Grace felt her anxiety levels rise. She'd completely forgotten about booking summer camps for the kids. It was hard enough trying to remember everything they might need for their upcoming trip.

"I'll look into it when we get back from Lakeview

OK? Thanks for reminding me though. Coffee when we return?"

After she and her friend exchanged a few more pleasantries, Grace replaced the receiver, and stood in the hallway rubbing her forehead.

Sometimes she felt as though motherhood was one huge roller coaster, with no breathing space at all in between. There was always something that the boys 'should' be doing, and for a moment she thought again of her plans to go back to college or the workplace, and wondered how she would juggle all of it.

"*Mum!*"

"*Mummy!*"

Grace looked at the top of the stairs and saw Jake and Josh standing there rubbing their eyes after their nap.

A few subtle differences helped to tell them apart. Josh had a small mole on his chin and Jake was a little bit taller.

At four years old, they still had that impish cuteness, but it was fading fast. They were growing up so quickly.

With a shriek, they ran down the stairs, taking two at a time and coming close to falling head first.

"Stop!" Grace cried, images of a screeching ambulance racing down their street on her mind. "You'll get hurt."

"Relax, it's just a little rough and tumble," Kevin said from behind her.

She glared at him. "Don't you know how dangerous those stairs are?"

"Grace, they're just being kids. Hello boys, give your daddy a big hug."

Kevin tickled each of the boys, until all three of them laughingly fell to the carpet.

Grace found herself smiling despite her panic. Kevin always had a way with them. She thought again of the looming trip and her smile froze.

She couldn't handle the twins by herself, they were just too much. Sometimes they could be sweet, but those times were now increasingly a rarity.

The majority of the time they were like twin tornadoes, destroying everything in their path.

"Go on in to the kitchen for your tea guys, Marie is waiting," she told them.

"But we want to eat our tea with you and daddy," Josh complained.

"Let them," Kevin said.

Grace sighed. "OK but you must promise to behave."

"Promise!" they chorused.

Grace went into their huge sunny kitchen and carried a tea tray to the living room.

Then she went back for the boys' milk and cookies. She placed their food on a square stool and arranged two small chairs opposite each other around it.

"Did you have a good day at work today?" she said to Kevin, enjoying the silence.

For a moment she felt at peace, the boys were eating their cookies quietly and she and Kevin could catch up, and they could all just be a family together.

But before her husband could answer, a quarrel arose.

"What is it?" she asked sharply, turning to the twins.

"It's Josh," Jake said. "Dipping his cookie in my milk. Disgusting."

"Stop it Josh, please," Grace said, feeling her blood pressure rising yet again.

"But mum, he did it first," Josh said in a whiny voice.

"I don't care who started, just eat quietly."

"You shouldn't let them get to you like that, hon. They're just being kids, let them be."

Grace deliberately picked up her tea and swallowed a huge sip, hoping to push down the eruption of annoyance. She didn't know how Kevin did it, keeping his cool with the boys like that. Most of the time they drove her so crazy, she couldn't think straight.

Like now.

She could see their feet kicking each other's shins under the stool. She tried to ignore it, but it felt like a pressure cooker, with the steam building every second.

Unable to bear it anymore, she put her cup on the table and stood up.

"I need some things from the shop; I'll just pop out and get them," she said and left.

How would she cope alone with them for a sustained period, Grace thought as she backed the car out of the garage.

If only Marie didn't have to travel back home.

She felt the tension leave her body as she drove and listened to jazz music coming from the speakers.

Their departure date was a week from now; still time to get used to the idea.

Or talk herself out of spending summer in Lakeview at all.

6

Marianne Cohen looked at herself critically in the bathroom mirror.

Her sleek long bob looked perfect, nothing was out of place. She leaned further towards it and looked at her face. Her skin had always been spotless, even when as teenagers her friends had been breaking out with acne, hers remained blissfully unaware of the raging hormones coursing through her veins.

Her lipstick needed retouching and she did this, giving the activity one hundred percent concentration, as she did with everything else. She took a step back and observed her reflection again.

Perfect.

Her black skirt suit and white shirt contrasted sharply with each other. She felt ready.

Marianne glanced at her wrist watch; it was nine o'clock, and she had thirty more minutes before her scheduled interview.

She gathered her folder and left the ladies room, walking confidently down the carpeted hall and through the glass doors that led to the office reception area.

"Morning Susan," she said cheerfully to the stern middle aged receptionist.

"Morning Marianne, you're early. Your meeting is not until half past."

"I know, I just like to be early. Oh and it's an interview, not a meeting."

"You've been with us for seven years, this doesn't really seem like an interview," Susan pointed out.

Marianne smiled and made her way to the black leather couches arranged around a glass table. She chose a seat that faced her boss's office.

"Tea?" the receptionist asked.

"Yes please."

A few minutes later, Susan placed a hot cup of tea on the table and Marianne murmured her thanks. She held the cup in both her hands as if for warmth, but the truth was that she was now feeling a little nervous.

The implications of this interview were huge. If

successful, Marianne's new post would be Head of Sales for the Dublin region.

Who would have thought she would end up working for a cosmetics company? She who had abhorred anything girly like make-up and any of that pink shrilly stuff that girls were supposed to like.

Growing up, she had fancied herself a boy like her three brothers and could kick a ball as high as they could.

Sitting in the plush office, Marianne realised how lucky she was. She had everything a woman in her late thirties would want. She had a great job and a wonderful husband, whom she adored and got along well with.

Her mood clouded a little. That wasn't quite right. They used to be happy together but these days, Donal did not seem to even remember she existed.

He was obsessed with work. The only thing he understood was ambition. Last night he had been even more nervous than she over this promotion.

When it came to work, Donal gave Marianne a hundred percent concentration. Take this morning. He had woken her up an hour earlier than usual and they had practiced the interview.

He had asked her all the possible questions that would come up. She had answered with confidence and knowledge, and now she felt sure that she would do well. Of course it was impossible to be completely at ease; after all, this was something that she really wanted.

"Marianne, I've told Ms. Walker that you're here and she'll see you now," Susan said.

She downed the rest of her tea and stood up to follow Susan into the office. Her boss was on the phone but when she saw Marianne, she waved her in.

Marianne sat down on the leather chair next to the desk. The office was medium sized but with rich furnishings and beautiful pieces of art hanging on each wall. Behind Ms. Walker's head was a glass wall that overlooked the city.

Her boss's fingers were adorned with gold rings, but her ring finger was bare. Marianne recalled that at all the end of year parties, Ms Walker attended alone and afterwards left alone in her darkened Mercedes. She always cut a figure of a recluse, but in meetings with clients she came alive, leading the conversation with witty insights and brilliant ideas.

For as long as she could remember, from the moment she started working here, Marianne had admired Ms. Walker. She was so focused and worked damn hard.

She was always the first to reach the office and the

last to leave for home. She was Marianne's beacon of hope and proof that hard work paid off.

Marianne wanted to follow in her footsteps and even surpass her achievements.

Who knew, perhaps one day, she would be the CEO of Prime Products.

She took this moment when Ms. Walker was engrossed in her conversation to look at her boss. She was very thin, fashionably so, with short hair that fell just below her jawline. In her late forties or even early fifties, it was hard to tell. She had aged well, but then she never drank, at least from what Marianne had observed at company parties, and she didn't smoke.

Now that she thought about it, Ms. Walker seemed to live a very austere life.

She was always here at the office, working at making Prime Products even more visible in the market. Rumour had it that she had a few shares in the company, and perhaps that's where her dedication stemmed from.

Marianne looked at her huge desk. There were no pictures of children or loved ones. Wait, there was one. But it was at an awkward angle and she couldn't quite see it.

When Ms. Walker swung her chair to face the glass window, Marianne reached for the photograph and tilted it her way. It was a picture of Ms. Walker holding a black and white tortoiseshell cat.

The picture was oddly disturbing, actually. She was a real mystery Ms. Walker. If the clues were correct, she lived her life entirely for Prime Products.

She looked at the picture again. It depicted quite a grim existence actually.

Was that cat all Ms. Walker had in the whole world? Who hugged her in the dead of the night when she got plagued by worry or sadness? Who did she talk about her day with in the evenings?

What about family?

Marianne considered the prospect of never having children and her heart constricted with pain. She had always wanted kids, but the timing was never right.

Maybe Ms. Walker had once been like her. Perhaps she too had wanted children but 'the timing was never right'?

Just then her boss finished her phone call and turned to Marianne, who gulped.

Show time.

7

That evening, as she prepared dinner for herself and Donal, Marianne realised what an uphill task faced her.

She had come to a realisation earlier in Ms Walker's office.

She remembered in the early days of their marriage, the feelings of giddy joy and absolute belief that this would be forever.

But people grew apart, a day at a time. These days Donal's work came first, or so it seemed.

Marianne admitted that for her, work was important, but after looking closely at her boss today she had seen that as important as it was, relationships were *the* most important.

And like gardens, they needed tending.

She and Donal had not tended theirs for a long time.

Donal was either on his laptop, or his phone. The only way to bring back the magic was to perhaps return to where it all started and try and recapture that?

Feeling excited at the thought of lazy days in the sun, Marianne poured sauce on top of the lasagne and slid it into the oven. She rinsed her hands and went to the dining table where her laptop was.

Their's was an open plan kitchen, chosen for the flexibility of cooking while talking.

A few clicks away and Marianne found the pretty little cottages in Lakeview, a huge improvement from the small rundown hotel they had first stayed in all those years ago.

These looked quaint and quiet, the perfect place for a couple to escape from the pressures of city life.

She browsed through several options until she found one that was right for them. Without giving it much thought, she filled out all the booking details, including her credit card details. Her hand lingered over the send key, and finally she hit it, and it was done.

Their summer retreat was booked.

. . .

DONAL WALKED IN AT SEVEN, holding a phone in one hand and a bag swinging from his shoulder. As he walked in, he finished talking on his phone and snapped it shut.

"Hi, welcome home," Marianne said.

"Hi yourself. I see from how happy you look that the interview went well?" he said his face creasing into the devastating smile that had first captured her attention way back in college.

"Interview?"

Donal looked at her puzzled. "Yes, interview, remember. The thing we woke up early this morning to practice for? The thing that you've been looking forward to."

"Oh, yes the interview. I'll tell you all about it over dinner," Marianne said without much enthusiasm.

He contemplated her for a moment, and then went into their bedroom down the corridor. Meanwhile, Marianne set the table for dinner, and brought out the lasagne. She also arranged wine glasses and took out a bottle of red wine from one of the kitchen cabinets.

Donal returned minus his jacket and tie, and the two top buttons of his shirt undone. He really was very handsome this husband of hers, Marianne thought.

She hadn't quite 'seen' him in years. It wasn't just his fault; she shouldered some of the blame too. She looked at him as a stranger might. He had black wavy hair, eyes that were green or blue depending on the angle of the sun, and full lips that were glorious to kiss.

He was tall and on the slim side, and he wore suits as though they were designed for his particular body alone. "What is it? You look like something's bothering you," Donal said.

"Nothing at all. Everything's fine."

Unconvinced, Donal sat down anyway and whistled at the wine. Usually they drank a few glasses of wine with their dinner on Friday or Saturday nights. Never on a Tuesday.

"Now I *know* the interview went well. Go on, spit out the good news. Is Marianne Cohen the new head of sales?" he asked, serving himself a slice of lasagne and scooping salad on to his plate.

"No."

"No?" Donal queried. "OK tell me what happened, because something obviously did."

"I never actually did the interview for the promotion. I cancelled it," she said.

Donal's eyes widened. "You did what? Why?"

"I went to Ms. Walker's office and sat down waiting for her to finish talking on the phone. I looked around her office, and Donal; there was not a single photograph of her with people she loved. There was only a picture of her holding her cat," Marianne said with feeling.

"So?"

"Can't you see, that's the price of success?" she said. "Honey, I don't want to live my life like that, alone with only a cat to love."

"But you have me, so that's unlikely."

"Maybe Ms. Walker had a husband too at one point and they divorced?" Marianne said. "And it seems to me that we are headed down that road too."

Donal put his fork down and stared at her. "*Divorce*? Am I missing something?"

"Haven't you noticed? We're so busy building our careers that we're neglecting our marriage."

Donal shifted about in his chair. "It's that way for many people these days though. You have to build your career and have a firm financial base. That's what we are doing."

Marianne looked at him with sadness and said nothing.

"So why did you cancel the interview?"

"I want a life Donal."

"You have a life," he said, ripping the napkin into tiny little pieces.

"I'm thirty seven years old, and I feel so alone yet I'm married."

He looked away.

"Look at me," she urged and when he did so she continued. "I love you and I want our marriage to work."

He was quiet for a while and Marianne crossed her fingers. She remained silent knowing that he usually needed time to think things through without being drowned with information.

"What do you want us to do so?" he finally said.

"I want us to go back to Lakeview. Remember that night all those years ago when you proposed; remember how romantic it was watching the moonlight over the lake, and just talking about our future?"

Donal looked wistful. "How can I forget?"

"So let's go back there - this summer."

Would he agree to take some time out together, back to Lakeview where he had proposed to her? Marianne closed her eyes and allowed herself to remember.

Back then, Donal had not acquired that distracted look he now wore all the time. He had taken her out on a boat on the lake and as they floated on the dark water, the moonlight casting shadows all around them, he had gone down on one knee and asked her to marry him.

"Well yes, I'm sure we will sometime but what about the job Marianne? Are you sure you don't want it?" Donal said sitting back to look at her face.

"I've never been so sure of anything."

"OK, but the perks would have been attractive," he pointed out, and Marianne knew he was testing her.

"Yes I know, but our marriage is more important, and maybe one day children too," she added quietly, before adding, "I booked us a cottage in Lakeview for the last two weeks in June."

Donal stared at her. "Are you serious?" he said. "You booked a holiday without consulting me?"

"I did, it's for us, we need this, Donal. We need time alone from everything."

"These things need to be planned. You can't just wake up one morning and decide you're going on holiday. I'm an investment consultant. There are people depending on me to make important decisions for them."

"Think about it though, we haven't had a holiday in TWO years. Come on you can do it. Remind them at work how long you've worked nonstop."

"It's not that. I have so much planned for the next

few weeks. There are meetings with clients and potential clients and conferences to attend. Ah, Marianne."

"I'm sorry; I know I shouldn't have booked it without speaking to you first." Marianne said, immediately contrite.

Donal inhaled deeply but said nothing. Then he sighed.

"OK it'll be tight, but if it's that important to you, maybe I can swing it."

Marianne threw herself on him and hugged him tight. Thank goodness. He really wanted to try; wanted their marriage to work as much as she did.

Then she thought of his mobile and laptop. Would he agree to switch them off while they were there though? Otherwise if he worked throughout, the break would be for nothing

Then she chided herself for her pessimism. Donal had agreed to go to Lakeview and that was the main thing.

One step at a time.

8

"We'll be fine, won't we boys?" Grace said in a cheerful voice, her hands gripping the steering wheel so hard that her palms hurt.

Kevin stood by the car, leaning on the driver's door.

"Drive safely, don't be in a rush," he reminded his wife, looking anxious. "I love you, have fun and I promise I'll pop down for a quick stay if I can," he assured her, and stepped away from the car.

"Love you too," Grace echoed, but she already knew that Kevin wouldn't be joining them.

Things had seriously heated up at the firm following the takeover, and he was working every hour God sent.

The last thing he needed was to sit in merciless summer traffic to and from Wicklow at the weekends.

She looked at the rearview mirror and for once the boys were uncharacteristically subdued.

"Are you OK guys?"

"I miss daddy, I want him to come with us," Jake pouted.

"It won't be any fun without daddy. I want to stay with *him*," Josh added.

"Well, you can't stay with daddy because he has to work. I explained all this to you already, didn't I? The three of us will go to Lakeview; we'll enjoy ourselves and come back home after a couple of weeks."

"I will *not* have fun," Jake said and crossed his arms across his chest.

"Me neither. I wish I wasn't going," Josh added.

Grace sighed. "You two sound very ungrateful, you know. A lot of kids would love to be in your situation, yet here you are sulking."

There was no response from the back seat and she looked at the mirror. They were looking out the window wearing sulky expressions.

Oh well.

It was two in the afternoon, and the sun was out in full force, glaring down and emitting a warmth that was almost too hot but not quite.

Grace drove with her window open and hummed along to the country music blaring from the radio. She glanced over at the boys and saw that they now were fast asleep. Jake's neck was at a funny angle and she worried as she looked at him.

Finally she pulled into a petrol station nearby and as she adjusted the position of his neck, he woke up. And Josh followed.

"I want to go wee-wee," he said.

"Me too.'

The three of them trooped to the bathroom which was on the other side of the station, next to a restaurant.

Grace shepherded them to the ladies' as she usually did when she was alone with them and there was no family toilet.

"I'm *not* going to a girl's toilet," Josh said stopping.

"Me neither. I want to go to the big boys' toilet."

"You can't go in there alone, you know that," Grace said.

She grabbed each twins' hand and tried to pull them in, but they wouldn't bulge. There was no one around, but still the thought of them entering the toilet alone petrified her.

"I'll buy you sweets in the shop next door," Grace

finally said, hating herself for backing down and resorting to bribes.

"Yaaay!" they yelled and followed her to the ladies toilet without further complaint.

Five minutes later, they were all back in the car, the twins happily sucking on their sweets. If Kevin had been there, he would not have needed to bribe them.

He had a way of talking that got the boys obeying what they were told. But as usual, she was useless at that, useless at everything when it came to her children.

Grace thought of the stay that lay ahead, and felt like bawling like a child herself.

9

It was mid-June, and summer had now begun in earnest.

At six in the morning, Ella headed over the stone bridge from her house to the café. Despite the early hour, the sun was already out in force, though the air was not as warm as it would get later, and already there were joggers running down the street.

She used her key to let herself in and closed it behind her. Summer opening hours were from seven to nine in the evening.

The inviting smell of coffee told her that Colm was already in. She crossed the empty dining room and entered the kitchen through a door behind the counter. Her chef was cutting up bacon, and when he heard footsteps, he turned to Ella with a smile.

"Good morning," he called out, waving the sharp knife he was using.

"I hope it *is* a good morning for you, I don't want that knife sticking out of me," Ella joked.

"Very funny. The coffee's ready if you want a cup."

"Thanks I will, but first let me get things started in here," she said, and went to the sink to wash her hands.

For the next hour, Ella arranged everything needed for the day. She and Colm worked in perfect unison, each following their own morning routine. The prep work done, she carried dishes from the kitchen to the dining room, setting breakfast cutlery on the counter, ready to be carried to individual tables.

At seven on the dot, Paddy Collins walked in, his walking stick making a tapping noise on the ground. He sat at his 'usual' table by the window.

Ella served him his tea and an omelet and as soon as she was finished, Sam the writer walked in. He had become a regular too over the last two weeks or so.

"Good morning." Ella greeted pleasantly.

"Morning to you too," he replied with a smile.

"What can I get you?" she asked, keeping the conversation short and to the point. She realised that the guy wasn't a big talker and didn't appreciate too much conversation, obviously liking his privacy.

"It's a bit empty in here this morning, isn't it?" Sam commented.

"Well," Ella started, wondering how to respond, "it's still a bit early. It's only seven."

"Oh is it?" he said, surprise in his voice. "Time loses all meaning when you're engrossed in something. I'll have a coffee and a doughnut please."

"Coming right up." Ella said, and walked away, bemused.

Perhaps his work was now coming along better then. He and Nina seemed to have struck up a friendship, and he had told her that he was under pressure to complete a novel while staying here, hence his need for privacy.

Ella poured out the coffee, and put a fresh doughnut on a plate, before carrying the lot to Sam. When she placed his breakfast on the table, he did not glance at her, his mind and eyes were on a spot somewhere across the street.

She soon forgot about him as other customers came in.

At a few minutes to eight, Nina started her shift and Ella retired to her office, a small room off the dining room.

Her rumbling stomach told her that she had

forgotten to have her morning coffee. She got up and went to serve herself coffee and a fruit.

Now Nina was talking to Sam, and for once he looked animated, even throwing his head back to laugh. Younger prettier women were obviously much more to his liking.

Smiling, Ella returned to her office with her coffee and a banana. She turned on her computer and made her usual biweekly orders.

She also took the time to update the books and then just when she was winding up, she heard a commotion coming from the café.

Quickly, she sprung from her chair and sprinted out of her office to the dining room. She got there just in time to see a woman yelling at her two children, who in turn looked petrified.

On the floor was a bowl of sugar, smashed into pieces.

Nina had already begun sweeping up the mess.

"Are you OK?" Ella said softly to the younger woman, who looked to be on the brink of tears. "Don't worry, it's just a sugar bowl and can be replaced."

"That's not the point," the woman said and this time *did* burst into tears.

By now they were the centre of attention.

"Come, let's go to out back, there's a playground

nearby," Ella murmured to the woman, then turned to the boys who were obviously twins. "Do you want to do something fun?" she asked and they yelled in response, making Ella want to close her ears with her hands. "Is that OK?" she asked the woman, who had not yet responded.

Instead, she nodded in reply as she wiped her tears and tried to regain her composure.

10

*E*lla held each boy by the hand and led them to a table on the outside patio.

She helped the woman, presumably their mother, sit down and then showed the boys to a playground in the park only a few steps away.

"They'll be safe there, it's entirely enclosed, not even a rabbit hole," she told her with a wink, and got a tentative smile in response. "Have you ordered anything?"

"I was just about to when—"

"That's OK; I'll get it for you. What would you like?"

"A cup of tea would be nice, and maybe two glasses of milk for the boys?"

"Coming right up," Ella said going back inside.

She felt sorry for her. Twins could overwhelm and that seemed to be exactly what was happening here.

She prepared the order, placed it on a tray and went back outside. The woman was still in the same position, under the parasol, although her attention was now on the boys.

"I can't believe how well they're playing without fighting or arguing or breaking something," she said, seemingly taken aback.

"Ah, kids that age just need to be kept busy."

After she placed the tray on the table, Ella sat down on the opposite chair and stuck out her hand.

"My name is Ella and I'm the manager here."

"Thanks. I'm Grace and the boys are Jake and Josh - they're four. Again I'm so sorry about the sugar. We came in for a treat, and hadn't even sat down - "

"Again, it's not a problem," Ella interjected pleasantly. "How do you tell them apart?"

"Josh is the one with the tiny mole on his chin."

They both turned their eyes on the boys who were engrossed in swinging beneath the sun.

Ella said nothing, just sat quietly, and as she had known, Grace begun talking.

For the thirty years that she had run the café, she had realised that most people wanted to talk, craved a sympathetic ear, and this woman was no different.

"We were supposed to come down here for two weeks with my husband Kevin, but at the last minute, he cancelled. Something came up at work, which he absolutely had to stay for. The boys' minder is away also, visiting her sick mother. And me ... well, I don't manage them so well on my own. We drive each other up the wall."

"Two at the same time are always a handful," Ella said but she could see that she had already lost Grace's attention.

"Jake, will you *stop* pushing him so high, what if he falls and breaks something?" she cried, a panicky note in her voice.

Ella was puzzled by her reaction. From what she could see neither boy was in any danger of getting hurt.

Besides, there was only so high the swing could go, and she pointed this out to Grace.

"See what I mean?" she said, throwing her hands in the air. "Even you, a stranger can see that I'm useless at this."

And she broke down into loud noisy sobs.

Ella rushed to her side and patted her back, murmuring soothing words. She looked over her shoulder at the twins, but luckily they were still absorbed with the swings, this time winding them round and round and then letting them go. She waited until Grace stopped crying and then returned to her chair.

"You know I remember my own son at that age, rushing round like a battery operated toy. Tons of energy all day like you've never seen. He was exhausting," she said, her eyes shining with the memory.

"Please tell me one day he stopped," Grace quipped with a moan, making Ella laugh.

"Not quite, however I did find a way to keep his energy levels down."

"What did you do?"

"I gave him freedom, mostly to play outside, under my supervision of course. Then either I or his dad played soccer with him, taught him how to ride a bike without stabilisers, took him swimming, hiking in the mountains ... the list is endless. They have so much energy, boys in particular," she added, her voice wistful.

Grace looked sceptical. "I wouldn't even know where to start with soccer."

"You could start by just getting a ball? These boys are four, you said? All they need at this stage is a ball to kick around, no fancy moves."

"OK, I suppose I'll give it a try," Grace said, but by

the tone of her voice, Ella doubted if she would. Still, she had done her bit by trying.

"I'd better go back inside," she said then. "Leave you three to enjoy your tea and milk."

"Again, I don't know what to say," Grace said with feeling. "Thank you very much for being so kind. About everything."

"It's no problem. And try not to worry. I have a feeling your boys will enjoy their time here in Lakeview," she assured Grace. "Most people do."

11

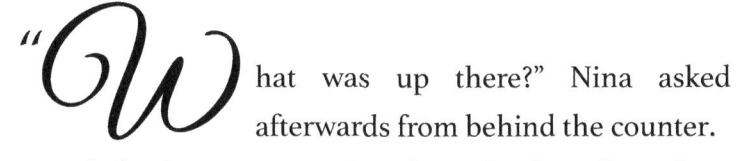

"What was up there?" Nina asked afterwards from behind the counter.

"Oh, she was just going through what all mothers do at one point or another. Being overwhelmed by kids."

Nina sighed. "Tell me about it."

"What do you mean?" Ella said turning to her in amazement. "Patrick is the best-behaved five-year old I know."

The other girl laughed. "No, you're right, he's good as gold. I was talking about Emma's," she said referring to her friend, Emma Harrington, another Lakeview mum. "He was over playing with Patrick yesterday and my bones are still aching. He has *way* too much energy."

Ella was thoughtful. "Mikey's about four now too, isn't he? Why don't you introduce yourself and Emma to Grace, the woman with the twin boys? That way the boys can have some playmates for the summer."

Nina was silent. "Look Ella, I know you mean well, but the summer tourists aren't always that friendly."

"Grace seems friendly."

Her colleague raised an eyebrow. "Not what I just saw when she was screeching at those poor boys."

"She was at her wits end, though."

Nina shrugged and Ella thought she seemed a little distracted regardless. "We'll see. I'd better get the order for that table."

But as Ella returned to the office, she realised that the table Nina was so eager to return to was none other than Sam's.

She watched for a moment, as the two of them laughed together at something.

Interesting...

Perhaps something other than coffee might be brewing in here this summer?

12

A few days later, in her Lakeview holiday cottage, Marianne stood at the upstairs window that overlooked the park.

She saw their neighbour, another summer tourist, and young mum who had introduced herself as Grace Carter. She seemed an anxious type, throwing nervous glances at her adorable twin boys.

Marianne watched them now at a distance, and she could see the two of them kicking a football.

Grace looked to be admonishing her sons about something, probably how far one of them had hit the ball.

She watched as the younger woman gestured with both hands, throwing back her long black hair with an impatient hand and storming off to get the ball.

Over the last few days since their arrival in Lakeview, she had seen Grace with her kids; and in truth it had now made Marianne a little more sceptical about having children.

This woman obviously struggled to handle her sons and she saw herself in Grace's shoes, wearing a permanent look of worry.

What kind of dad would Donal make either, with his phone almost always attached to his ear?

She could hear him now downstairs, giving instructions to someone in the office. They hadn't exchanged more than good morning.

He had woken up much earlier, and when Marianne got up, she found him sitting in the dining table working on his laptop.

He had waved to her without even glancing her way.

Marianne sighed. Their romantic summer break was not so far turning out as she had anticipated.

Her attention snapped back to the scene at the park when she heard a sharp cry. Grace stood clutching a ball with one hand, and gesturing with the other. One of the boys was with her and Marianne felt her insides tense when she couldn't immediately see the other twin.

Her eyes scanned the area and that's when she saw

him - behind a tree, squatting beside the grass, looking intently at something. He was out of his mother's view, and she was clearly frantic looking for him.

Marianne left her spot and rushed downstairs, taking the steps two at a time. She didn't tell Donal where she was going; he wouldn't even know she was gone, she figured.

Outside she jogged all the way into the park, reaching Grace as fast as she could.

"Hi there," Marianne said, trying to catch her breath.

'I can't find Josh!" Grace cried, her eyes wide with fear.

"I know, I saw from my window," Marianne said, speaking fast. "He's OK; he's just behind that tree over there."

Grace sprinted towards the huge oak tree that she pointed to and returned shortly holding Josh's hand. He looked happy and contented, unaware of any worry he had caused.

"Don't *ever* go off like that without telling me," Grace ordered.

"I was just looking at an insect," Josh said and shrugged his mother's hand off.

Grace was white as a sheet, and looking at her closely, Marianne saw that she was shaking.

"I told Kevin that I couldn't do this alone. It's so hard."

"Do what?" Marianne said, interested.

Grace looked at her then, as if noticing her presence for the first time.

"I'm so sorry ... thanks for helping. I was going mad with worry; I thought someone had stolen him."

Then to Marianne's shock, Grace broke down into silent sobs.

She glanced at the boys but they had gone back to playing with the ball.

Awkwardly, Marianne pulled the other woman into a hug. She was much taller, but at the moment, she just looked defeated.

She felt sorry for her but wondered why two little boys overwhelmed her so much.

They were just kids after all.

13

"Marianne!" a voice called out then. It was Donal and he was walking towards them. "Why didn't you say you were going out?" he said, sounding irritated.

"I thought you'd be too busy to notice I was gone," she retorted.

He glared at her and then his eyes shifted to Grace.

"This is Grace, our neighbour and those are her two boys. Grace this is my husband Donal," Marianne said. "I came to help her find one of the boys."

Shakily, Grace stretched out a hand. "Your wife has been wonderful. I was going mad with worry." She turned to Marianne again. "Thank you so much."

She looked like she would burst into tears again at any moment. Marianne felt sorry for her, and wondered what kind of husband would let his wife and kids go off to a strange place alone.

"Tell you what Grace, why don't you head on back to your cottage and take some time for yourself?" she offered, before she could think about it. "Donal and I will watch the boys for a little while," she said, touching Grace lightly on the shoulder.

"What? Oh... I don't know. I'm sure you have your own day planned out," Grace said, though Marianne could tell that the other woman desperately wanted to take up her offer.

"We'd love to, besides, it will be good practice for when we have our own," she joked, glancing at Donal who gave her a blank stare.

"To be honest, I feel as if I could really use a break," Grace conceded with that nervous way she had of smiling. "Let me just tell the boys."

"Great. And we can take them over to the cafe later for a snack if that's OK."

"Sounds brilliant. You are so kind. Thanks again."

"Are you *insane*?" Donal said as soon as Grace was out of earshot.

"What? Why?"

"Why would you volunteer to watch over some strange woman's kids?" he said tersely.

"If you took your nose out of your laptop for a

moment, you'd know that she wasn't strange woman, but our next door neighbour," Marianne said between gritted teeth.

Donal looked away moodily and then said, "I thought you wanted a romantic getaway for the two of us."

Marianne closed her eyes and counted to ten. When she opened them, Grace was back with the two boys.

"These are our neighbours, Mr. and Mrs. Cohen, and they're going to watch you for the rest of the morning. Be respectful now, boys," she said, then turned to Marianne and Donal. "I'll just be in the house taking a breather. Don't hesitate to drop them back if they're too much trouble."

"Don't worry one bit." Marianne assured her. "We've got this under control."

14

Nina looked out the window of her and Patrick's little flat on Main Street, hardly unable to believe what she was seeing.

Her breath caught as she smiled at the scene before her. Sam was teaching Patrick how to use a skipping rope. The two of them were laughing and clearly enjoying themselves.

The hair on the top of Sam's head was standing as it usually did, and Nina felt an urge to run her fingers through it.

Since his arrival, she and Sam had struck up somewhat of a friendship during his time at the cafe.

Though Nina had been hesitant to talk to him initially, since he was like a yoyo with his mood changes. Sometimes he wanted conversation, other times not.

He and Patrick played for a few more minutes and she saw Sam look up at the window.

She swallowed hard when their gazes met. He had the most arresting eyes she had ever seen. They were almond-shaped and grey, a colour that either lightened or darkened depending on his mood.

She reacted like that a lot these days whenever she saw Sam.

He had sharp cheekbones and lips that were perfectly shaped, possibly resembling those handsome heroes he wrote about in his books.

To her embarrassment, Nina had roamed the local bookshop looking for one of his novels. He was a brilliant writer, there was no doubt about that, but the type of thriller stories he wrote about were not quite to her taste.

Now she waved and quickly went downstairs to join them.

"Aren't you the active one?" she said, smiling broadly.

"That's my exercise for the day done," he grinned before adding. "Any chance of a cuppa?"

"I can even do better than that, I can make you

brunch if you like," she suggested, her heart beating faster that norm. "Patrick and I were just about to eat."

"That would be brilliant, thanks," Sam said, following her upstairs to her small two bed flat.

Nina knew why the palms of her hands were sweaty and her body was tense. It was embarrassing, and she had promised herself that nobody including Sam would ever know.

She had a major crush.

Initially, she had told herself that perhaps it was because he was a celebrity of sorts, but that reason didn't hold much water. After all, when he first came to town she had no idea who he was.

At the cafe, she could look at him all day without getting bored. He was handsome but more than that, his face was like a changing landscape.

It reflected whatever mood he was in. Sometimes his features were tight and tense, and when he was happy, like now, his face glowed.

Nina busied herself frying eggs and bacon, and when they were ready; she popped two slices of bread in the toaster.

Tea was ready and she poured two cups, and sat down opposite Sam at the table. She almost jumped when their knees touched, but she managed to calm herself down.

"How's the book going these days?" she asked, sipping on her tea while cutting up bacon for Patrick.

"Good actually, much better than expected. If it continues moving at that pace, I may be gone before summer is up."

"Might be time for a break then," she said, her heart dropping a little. "Patrick and I are going for a walk around the lake trail after this, want to come?" She tried to sound casual. "It's too beautiful a day to stay cooped up inside."

Sam looked up in surprise. He seemed to contemplate this for a moment, and she wanted to shrink into the ground at that very moment.

What had made her open her big mouth?

"Sounds like a great idea. I'd love to see a bit more of the place, actually."

Nina tried her utmost not to grin like an idiot.

15

"Do you know how to play football?" one of the twins asked Donal. "My dad does."

Donal looked at Marianne and she shrugged. Let him handle this one.

"Course I know. Spread out, let's kick to each other," he said, and then whispered to Marianne. "I mean, I know how soccer is played, not that I'm any good at it."

She smiled. "I'll just sit here on the grass and watch. Here, give me your phone; I'll hold it for you," she offered.

He was surprisingly good with the kids and soon had them screaming and cheering.

"Don't forget to call me if my phone rings," he called out after a little while and she mouthed 'OK'.

She felt a twinge of guilt at actually having switched it off, but shook it away. They were on holiday weren't they?

Donal had no business working full time while they were here. Besides he was breaking his side of the bargain.

He had promised to spend quality time with her, yet every day so far, was putting in more or less the same hours at work as he did back home.

They played for about an hour, after which Donal collapsed on the ground beside his wife. His pale demeanour had left, in its place glowing skin and twinkling eyes.

Despite himself, he was enjoying himself.

"Will you play hide and seek with us?" one of the twins asked then. Marianne still couldn't tell who was who.

"Sure I'd love to." She stood up and followed the little boy to where the other twin was waiting.

"I'll count first and you boys hide," she said. "But not too far away, mind you. We don't want anyone getting lost."

She turned away from them, stood against a towering elm tree, and buried her head in her folded arms.

"One, two..."

When Marianne reached twenty and all was quiet, she tentatively lifted her head, and when she saw no one she started searching.

She found Josh first, hiding behind a tree, and they raced together to see who would tap the tree first.

Josh got there and Marianne feigned disappointment. She found Jake and Donal next, hiding behind a rubbish bin.

To Marianne's surprise, she found herself laughing out loud at the boys' antics and enjoying herself.

It was nice to be silly and not have a care in the world.

16

Marianne played with the twins for another half hour or so, and soon she could see the boys were getting worn out.

Not to mention poor old Donal too.

"Let's go to the cafe for a bite and a drink," she suggested.

"Yay!" The boys cried out in unison.

"Let's go then, my treat," Donal said. "Give me my phone, honey."

Without giving it a second thought, Marianne reached into the pocket of her denim shorts and handed the device to him.

"It's off. I could have sworn it was fully charged," he frowned.

She shrugged. "I switched it off."

"What? Why did you do that? You know how important it is that I keep abreast with what's happening at the office," he said tightly.

"Let's go boys," Marianne shepherded the boys ahead towards Ella's cafe.

When they were out of earshot, she scowled at Donal. "I'm tired of this; in fact if you're that worried about work, go on then, back to your 'office' right this minute."

She knew she had a temper, but she never got a warning or felt it coming. It was like an undetected tornado.

Once in the grip of it, she recognised it and most times managed to calm herself down. But now she felt so fed up, she could have howled in frustration.

Donal looked duly taken aback. "Hey, calm down, what is all this about?"

"It's about you and your unwillingness to leave your work behind," Marianne hissed. "The idea of coming here was to spend time together."

"We *are* spending time together."

"No we are not. You wake up early every day and work on your laptop most of the morning!"

"But we always have lunch together and spend afternoons together," Donal said, confused.

"No, we might have lunch in the same spot but we

are never together. You're always on your phone as you eat, or while we take walks in the afternoon. What's the point?"

Being so close to lunchtime, the cafe was packed, but there was one table on the outside patio area.

The boys went with them to the table, but then raced over towards the swings while they waited.

"They have so much energy," Donal commented.

Marianne was still too annoyed to respond.

Ella came over to serve them. "Hello Donal and Marianne," she greeted with a smile. They'd eaten here almost every days since their arrival and were on first name terms with the friendly host.

"Hi," they both echoed. Marianne felt embarrassed that today neither of them bothered to hide that fact that they were fighting.

Of course Ella must surely have come across fighting couples before, not that it was much of a comfort.

"Are you watching the twins for Grace today?" she asked.

"Yes, she was a bit overwhelmed earlier, so we said we'd take them for a couple of hours. Do you have something they can eat?"

"Yes, they love milk and Colm's cookies or Twix cake. What about you two?"

"Sounds good. I'll give the Twix cake a try too. And some tea please," Marianne asked.

"I'll have the same."

"Great, I'll be back soon."

The tension between them was so thick, you could cut it with a knife. Right this moment, Marianne was sure that Donal had no idea what the big deal was.

He was so clueless sometimes, but for now she wasn't budging and would not, until he understood for himself what the matter was.

Ella duly returned with their order, and Marianne called out to the twins to come back and wash their hands.

They settled down to eat; the boys chattering aimlessly about nothing in particular.

They were good kids, she thought.

Under the table Marianne felt rather than saw their little feet kicking each other. She smiled, remembering that she used to do the same thing with her sister Carina when growing up.

She hid a smile and continued with her meal, pretending not to notice what the kids were doing under the table.

Sometimes they would erupt into giggles and she laughed too at the joy of hearing the laughter of children. It made her feel another sharp longing for one of her own.

The boys finished their milk and cake, and as Marianne was gathering their plates and cups together, she looked up and saw Grace, standing from a distance, at the other edge of the patio.

The look on her face made Marianne freeze. Her hair looked wild, like she had woken up without combing it. But her eyes were even wilder, and her body was so still; Marianne wondered how long she had been standing there.

She was just about to wave over, when one of the kids caught her attention, and she looked away for a moment.

But when Marianne turned back to the boys' mum to beckon her inside to join them, Grace was gone.

17

The weather was warm that afternoon, with a slight breeze blowing off the lake.

For their walk, Nina had changed clothes and wore a pair of loose shorts and a sports t-shirt that emphasised her slim body.

Little Patrick was also in shorts and a t-shirt, while Sam wore his relaxed writer 'uniform' of light canvas trousers and a linen shirt.

She guessed that they looked like the perfect family, a little boy skipping happily along the path, his parents strolling casually behind him.

She still couldn't believe that she had worked up the courage to invite Sam like this.

They walked leisurely along the lake through the park, shaded by swaying trees. The trail route began near the inside shores of the lake and turned upwards towards the Wicklow hills.

She loved this woodland part of Lakeview more than the lake, which was the bigger tourist draw. It was so peaceful.

"I'd love to experience snow in these parts," Sam said, looking around at the rolling hills and forestry. "I'd say it's even more spectacular."

"Yes, winter up here has its own kind of beauty." Nina said, picturing the ice-covered trees and houses and pine trees sprinkled with snow. "It's so quiet in the town, and hauntingly beautiful in the woods in particular."

"The best time of the year, I reckon."

Nina smiled. Sam was a kindred spirit. Most people complained about the winter in Ireland, the damp cold and howling winds, but for Nina, that time of year also held a different kind of appeal.

Lakeview was much quieter absent of tourists, and there was a certain comfort in seeing the same familiar faces every day.

Just when they turned the corner at the far end of the lake, Nina heard her name called out from behind.

It was Emma Harrington in the park, walking towards her and holding her little boy Mikey's hand.

Nina smiled and waited for her friend to reach

where they stood. The sun light was almost like a halo behind her head, her glossy hair bouncing as she walked.

Emma was unattached and gorgeous, and while the two were good friends, having bonded over their shared single-mum status, now the other girl's effortless glamour made Nina feel like a bag lady in front of Sam.

"Hello there," Emma greeted when she got closer. "Where are you all off to?"

"Just taking a walk along the trail. You're welcome to join us, if you like," Nina added out of politeness, though she sorely hoped her friend would refuse.

Emma wasn't keen on exertion most of the time, so Nina didn't think hiking would be her scene.

"Oh great," Emma replied, flashing Sam a sidelong smile. "We were just heading down the town for a wander but a little adventure would be fun."

Mikey and Patrick walked on ahead, the three adults following closely behind. There was not enough space on the trail-path for the three to walk together, so Nina fell behind a step Sam and Emma.

She took this time to watch Sam. She loved the way he tilted his head slightly to speak to someone, and the way he threw his head back when he laughed.

Which he was doing a lot with Emma, Nina realised, her heart twisting a little.

18

Stone steps led to the top of the hill, and the beginning of the trail proper.

Pine trees flanked the thin pathway on either side, creating the dramatic effect of entering a darkened cave. Even though they had been here more times than Nina could count, the kids giggled as they followed her inside. The darkened effect came from leaving a well-lit area to a shaded area, and soon their eyes adjusted to the light.

"Hey boys, anyone know the names of these trees?" Nina asked, referring to some broad-leafed trees on the left side.

"I do, Mum," Mikey yelled from behind. "They're called elms."

"Correct, well done. And who knows when this trail was completed?" she continued.

"I do." Sam's deep voice replied.

She kept up the string of questions as they walked. Giggles and shouts were heard, when someone fell behind or tripped. Nina loved to do this, ask questions about the trail, it kept the kids busy and occupied and maintained their interest in nature.

She stopped when they reached the small wooden bridge that went over a little stream. It was almost dry now but if you came during winter, flowing water rushed down, all the way to the lake.

Emma and Sam still seemed deep in conversation, about Sam's writing life, it seemed.

"Sometimes it's a pain," Sam was saying. "Like now, I have a character who is into river rafting, something I've never done."

"I could take you river rafting," Emma offered quickly. "We do a lot of that around these parts."

"I didn't say it's something I want to try," Sam joked.

"Coward," she teased.

They were obviously flirting, which made Nina feel stupid now. Of course someone like Sam would be *way* more interested in the likes of Emma.

Why had she even thought to assume any different? And maybe she was dreaming too, but she'd never once heard Emma mention anything about ever going river rafting.

"What do you think Nina - should I give it a go?" Sam asked then, turning to look at her and giving her a penetrating look that made her legs feel like they were made of water.

She pretended to give it a lot of thought.

"You should, it's not hard at all. A little scary at first, but if you have a weak stomach maybe it's not the greatest idea, because you'll get tossed and turned like a washing machine."

Sam beat his hard midsection with his hand. "My stomach can handle it."

"In that case give it a shot. You can't be here and not try rafting once. And I'm sure it would be good for research."

"OK, you've convinced me, I will."

Nina saw the way Emma's eyes lit up at this, and knew for sure that her friend fancied him. "Perfect. It's a date, then. Don't worry, it'll be fun, I'll make sure of it."

Nina's heart fell into the pit of her stomach now. She grabbed the boys by the hand, and they continued walking.

Further on, they came to her favourite spot on the

trail - the meadow at the top of the hills. Up here, the grass was an almost translucent green, and grew so long in some places an adult could hide unseen.

Yellow butterflies could be seen flying from one long grass to another, or landing on the multicoloured flowers, merging with the flower completely so that you couldn't tell which was butterfly or flower. The kids broke into a run, chasing the butterflies in the long grass.

"You can't see this at all from back there," Sam said his voice filled with awe.

Nina felt her heart swell with pride, as though she was responsible for the presence of the meadow. She loved the surprise in visitor's voices when they first saw the place. "Sometimes you even get to see deer roaming about."

"It just looks so ... natural and untouched," Sam said.

"It is. These days it's protected, but back in the olden days, farmers used it to graze their cattle and sheep. The meadow gets its water from the river water tributaries, which run underground, hence its greenness and beauty all year round."

"You're really good at this stuff Nina, have you ever considered becoming a tour guide?" Sam asked.

She found herself blushing.

"I always tell her the same thing. Nina would make a fantastic tour guide; she's kinda the town historian too," Emma joked.

Nina bristled a little. Why did her friend have to expose her secret dreams like that?

She had once confided in Emma that she might like to work in tourism. Now Sam was in on it too, and Nina couldn't explain the fear she felt at the thought of going back to work full-time.

"Ah, where would I get the time to do something like that?" she replied and found herself squirming under Sam's stare.

"Honestly. You have a real talent for this sort of thing Nina, don't waste it," he said solemnly.

Perhaps he was right, but something held her back from pursuing her dreams. And that little something was scrambling ahead of them as they walked.

After a little while, they headed back down the trail, but this time, Nina was very quiet.

Her mind swirled with the possibilities. For the first time in years, she felt herself growing braver, and thinking how her life would be if she went back into the workplace proper. She enjoyed waitressing for Ella now and again, but the truth was that she mostly did it for extra money and the chance to get out and about.

Who knew maybe someday, she would think about

a career and what would happen when her son got older and didn't need her so much any more.

But that was some way off, so for now, Nina would concentrate on what she'd promised to do right from the very beginning, be the best mother to Patrick that she could.

19

Ella shepherded Grace into the café, and guided her across the room, down the hallway to her office.

The younger woman was like a docile doll, and she followed her willingly.

"You look as white as a sheet," Ella commented, when they'd sat down. "What is it?"

In response, Grace buried her head in her hands.

"I had a scary moment in the park this morning when I thought I'd lost Josh. Turns out he was behind a tree all along, and it was Marianne who found him. She and her husband volunteered to watch the boys for a bit this afternoon to give me a break."

"That was kind. They're lovely people."

"Yes they are. I went back home and dozed off a

little, and when I woke up they were nowhere to be found. They were not at the park or at the house. I'd forgotten that Marianne mentioned they might take them here for a treat." Her bottom lip quivered. "I ... I thought they'd kidnapped them and all I could think was - what would I tell Kevin? That I was so selfish for my time that I gave the boys to total strangers?"

"Aren't they your neighbours though?" Ella pointed out. "Summer visitors at the cottages always end up mixing while on a stay here. Nothing selfish about that."

"Yes, but look at how content and happy the boys look with them out there? They're *never* like that with me," their mother sniffed.

Ella smiled reassuringly and contemplated sharing her true thoughts.

Someone needed to talk to this woman otherwise she would drive herself crazy.

"Love, you can't think like that. It's nothing personal. They're enjoying the novelty of having someone else take care of them in a different place. They are typical kids; all they want is food, a little discipline and the space to play."

"But I *do* all that for them, don't I?" Grace mumbled.

"Yes, but based on what I've seen, you're such a

bundle of nerves with them, it's almost like ... like they're not your kids?" Ella stated.

She didn't want to be harsh, but the poor woman was obviously struggling, and she needed to help her put things in perspective.

Grace looked at her, startled. "Of course they're mine."

"Oh I know that, but you're so worried about them all the time, it's almost like they've been foisted on you."

Grace sighed. "Well, right from the beginning when we first found out we were having twins, all anybody told me was how much more difficult and troublesome things were going to be. And I suppose that's always how I've viewed them, as just a lot of additional hassle." She shook her head. "To be honest, I've never really handled them all by myself like this. There's always been the nanny, and Kevin of course. He's great with them. You're right though - sometimes even *I* feel like they are strangers."

"Well, why don't you try to get know them better then?" Ella said, but she could see Grace's mind had already wandered.

"If only Kevin could manage to come down even for a couple of days... Maybe if I tell him how exhausted I am..." She stood up. "In the meantime, I'd better go and rescue Marianne and Donal - I'm sure they're exhausted for sure." She gave a nervous laugh.

Ella shook her head.

Evidently, this young mother had convinced herself a long time ago that her twins were nothing but trouble, and seemed there was no persuading her otherwise.

20

The following day, Nina was standing behind the counter catching her breath after the lunchtime rush.

"Penny for your thoughts?" Ella asked, having noticed that the younger girl seemed preoccupied these days.

Nina smiled. "They are definitely not worth that much."

"How's your dad?" she probed.

"He's great - watching Patrick today actually."

"It's so cute how much he adores him."

"How much they adore each other. Which is a turn up for the books..." Nina added with a mirthless laugh, obviously thinking about how her pregnancy had initially been very difficult for her father to process and had caused major upheavals in both their lives.

Thankfully their relationship had come on leaps and bounds since Patrick was born.

Ella was concerned though. Nina was typically a jolly person, but lately she seemed more subdued.

"Are you OK? You've been kind of quiet these days."

The younger woman looked at her and smiled brightly. "I'm fine, everything's just fine," she said and picked up a cloth for wiping the tables.

Ella shrugged. If Nina had something to share she guessed she would do so when she was good and ready.

She went outside to the patio area, to see if any customers needed attending to. There was a couple lingering beneath a parasol on one of the tables, and Marianne was sitting at another.

To Ella's surprise, she looked to be crying, although it seemed she was trying hard not to.

Oh dear.

Moving quickly, she headed over and slid onto the chair alongside her.

"Are you OK sweetheart?" Ella asked, concerned. "Where's Donal?"

Marianne blew her nose and attempted to repair

her face by wiping the mascara dripping down her cheeks.

"He's at the cottage. I'm OK, really."

"You know it does help to talk it out," Ella coaxed, smiling gently.

Marianne looked so sad now, as though she carried the weight of the whole world on her shoulders.

She was young too, probably only in her late thirties.

What could be so terrible, Ella wondered, especially when in the short time she'd known her she always seemed so cheery.

"Just tell me what's bothering you," she urged her. "I'm sure whatever it is, it can't be that bad."

21

"I ... I think my marriage is in trouble Ella, no—I *know* it is. Donal is just not the person I married nearly ten years ago," Marianne sniffed then.

"Of course he's not the same person, love. People change over time," Ella pointed out.

"Do you know he proposed right here in Lakeview, out on the lake, under a full moon," Marianne continued, her eyes brimming with the memories of that time. "We were so in love back then, we saw nothing but each other."

"You were here? Ten years ago?" Ella scratched at her memory for their faces but so many tourists had come and gone in the interim....

Or perhaps she was just growing old, she thought with a wry smile.

"Donal is obsessed with work, and he's forgotten about us. Coming back here was my chance to get him to see what's happening. I want us to have children, but at the moment that's such a far-fetched dream...." Marianne's voice faded away.

It was difficult. Ella knew the pitfalls of being career focused. People lost track of so much else in the search for success.

"What were your goals when you got married? As a couple?" she asked.

Marianne was silent as she contemplated her question. Ella took this time to look at her properly.

She had cover girl pretty looks, with sleek hair that fell to her shoulders. Ella had noticed that Marianne always had her make up perfectly applied, and was constantly well-dressed, even in casual wear.

But more than that, she had a good heart. Look how she had volunteered to watch Grace's twin boys that time?

"We wanted to work hard, and build our lives. We were just starting out in our careers and had nothing to our names, so success was a big goal. For one, we wanted to buy an apartment in a good part of Dublin, which we have. Secondly, both of us wanted to climb the corporate ladder in our respective companies."

"And have you?"

"Almost. Donal wants to reach to the very top, and as for me, just before we came here, I had been invited to interview for a big promotion."

Marianne went on to narrate to Ella the events of the day she had cancelled the interview with Ms Walker.

"OK, so he might be ambitious but love, from where I'm standing, I'd say Donal hasn't done anything wrong," Ella pointed out.

Marianne turned to her in disbelief. "How can you say that after everything I've just told you? We came back here to try recapture our romance. Donal just doesn't get that there are more important things than work."

"What I mean," Ella clarified, "is that Donal hasn't moved the goalposts, but you have. You told me yourself that when you got married your goals at the time were to achieve success. Perhaps you feel that you've already done that but clearly Donal hasn't. Seems that *you're* the one who decided that you want out of the race now. As far as he's concerned, the two of you are still chasing promotions and looking to climb the corporate ladder, and why would he think otherwise?"

After a long moment, Marianne looked at her unblinking. "I think I see what you mean. I've changed, and I'm expecting Donal to suddenly change as well."

"Don't get me wrong," Ella said. "He is also being a little thoughtless. The two of you do need to spend quality time together, after all that's what holidays are for. To bond and remember why you're together. So he's not entirely off the hook." She smiled." I'm just trying to be devil's advocate, try and see things from his point of view. So perhaps we should try to wear his shoes for a moment and look at things as he might?"

They were both quiet, and Ella knew that Marianne was trying to absorb all that she had told her.

After several minutes, she spoke again. "What can I do, what's the way forward for us now in our marriage, if our life goals are suddenly so different?"

Ella laughed softly. She wished things were as simple as that. Marriage was not like the workplace, where colleagues could sit down together in the conference room and brainstorm.

"I wish I knew. This one you have to work out for yourself. I'm sure you will though."

"How do you know that?"

"Because you've already done the most important thing," Ella said, standing up.

"Ah, don't leave me in the dark like this," Marianne pleaded.

"You've shifted your outlook. You understand his side of the story. You know why he's the way he is, and it's definitely nothing personal. What you have to figure out now is the best way forward for both of you."

With that, and a parting squeeze on the younger girl's shoulder, Ella glided away and back inside the cafe.

22

"Mummy can we go outside?" Josh pleaded.

"Mummy, look what I can do…" Jake demanded.

Grace's head throbbed, and felt like it would explode. She wiped the cottage countertop with force, hoping to transfer all her negative feelings to the marble kitchen counter.

"Mummy, can we go swimming—"

"*Mummy!!*"

They started again, their voices rising as if in competition to see who would speak loudest.

To Grace, their voices sounded like hammers banging mercilessly inside her brain.

"We can't do either of those things, firstly because I need to finish cleaning up the house first, and secondly, Josh you know that mummy can't swim and daddy's not here to take you to the pool," Grace said, hoping that was the end of it.

"We want to go swimming…" the boys chanted in unison, coming nearer.

"Just… please…stop it!"

Her loud voice shocked them into silence. Horrified, Grace dropped the cloth, and raced out of the room.

Going upstairs she went to her room and threw herself face down on the double bed.

She let the tears come. Why was it so difficult for her to manage them? They were her children for crying out loud! She more than anyone else, should know them by now.

When her cries subsided, she thought back to when the boys were in the cafe with Marianne.

They had all seemed so relaxed.

What had so upset her that day was Marianne's behaviour when the boys had started kicking their feet under the table.

She had just laughed and let them be. Grace's own reaction would have been anxiety that they'd hurt each other, cause a commotion, or break something.

She knew she overreacted, Kevin had told that her enough times. But hearing it from strangers too, like the nice café owner, she felt that there maybe was something there.

Now Grace viewed her moments with the boys in flash shots since they'd come to Lakeview.

That first day at the café when a sugar bowl had broken, making her shout at them. Then running off at the sight of them having fun with Marianne and Donal.

People here must think she was crazy. She remembered how on both occasions, Ella had shepherded her away and listened to Grace while she ranted.

Another clear image of her at the park, searching frantically for her son before Marianne came along and uncovered his hiding place, and yet again Grace had bawled like a baby.

She cringed at how quickly she had just handed her boys over to people she barely knew, just to get away from that feeling of being overwhelmed.

Grace sighed. When had all this started? And why did she notice it here more than back home?

Sure there was Kevin and Marie, but as their mother, she still spent a considerable amount of time with the boys, driving them to and from pre-school, and from one sport or activity to another.

It hit her then. Every last one of her friends was the same. They were all rushing through the days as though expecting a tornado to come crushing into them at any moment.

In a moment of stark clarity, Grace realised that motherhood had always seemed like one huge competition, a huge undertaking.

Which child had more skills? Which mummy signed up their offspring for more activities?

Just thinking about it now made her feel exhausted.

The group of women she called her friends were the very same as she was, a bunch of anxious worried mums.

That was no way to live. It was tiresome and it robbed you of the capacity to enjoy life.

Look at her now. She was in the most beautiful tourist town and she couldn't relax or even enjoy the long days of summer with her boys.

She missed Kevin too. The trip would have turned out so much different if he had been with them.

Feeling the threat of self-pity, Grace jumped from the bed. She thought of her twins bored downstairs and quickly galvanised herself into action.

The house could be cleaned some other time.

"Boys?" she yelled from the top of the stairs. "Come on up and pack your things—we're going swimming."

Two faces appeared at the bottom, staring at Grace with hopeful eyes. She felt her heart melt at how sweet they looked just then.

"Yes that's right, we're going to the pool," she repeated, ignoring the anxious flutter that had already begun in her tummy.

They boys usually played around in baby pools in Dublin where the water went up to their waists, and for Grace, it would probably reach below her knees.

No swimming skills were necessary.

She knew there was a leisure centre in Lakeview but didn't know if it had a kids' pool. Her body went stiff at the thought of the boys in an adult pool.

They were so boisterous, what if one of them ran off without her seeing and fell into the deep end?

Grace didn't know how to swim, so she would only be able to watch helplessly as her boy drunk mouthfuls of water, his panicky eyes wide, until he disappeared into the bottom of the water …

Oh God. Why was this so hard?

23

Ella's tummy was rumbling with hunger. She glanced at her wristwatch.

Late afternoon, and she hadn't had a bite to eat since breakfast. This happened often; she got so carried away with her work or talking to customers that she forgot to eat.

She went into the kitchen, and finding a pile of dishes and Colm busy, decided to tackle those first.

The dishwasher was misbehaving, so she filled the sink with water and one by one washed off the grease.

Half an hour later, she was finished, and the kitchen looked half decent again. She made herself a beef sandwich and went out to the counter for a cup of coffee.

That done, she carried her lunch to a table by the window.

She chewed on her sandwich as she watched people walk past. From her vantage point she could see the shops across the street and people going in and out.

Summer was a great time for the town, and Lakeview continued to grow exponentially year on year.

There was talk of a new tourist centre being built soon, and Ella crossed her fingers that it would happen.

Soon, she felt rather than saw the presence of someone nearby and looked up in surprise to find Nina on the chair alongside her, still wearing that thoughtful faraway look on her face. "Hello there."

"Hello back," Nina grinned. "I suppose you're wondering what I'm doing here interrupting your lunch."

Ella looked at her, swallowed a mouthful of sandwich and said, "No. I was just thinking how lovely it is of you to join me. It's always lonely eating alone."

Nina laughed. "I love you Ella, I really do. Anyway, I wanted to ask you something, a kind of rhetorical question."

"The best kind," she replied. "I'm good at rhetorical questions."

"Have you ever had a summer romance?"

Ella hid a smile. Even before Nina uttered another word, she could guess what - or more to the point *who* - was at the heart of this conversation.

Sam the writer.

"I have. A long time ago," Ella said, not mentioning that the affair in question was with a man who eventually ended up being her husband.

It had been summertime when she'd first come to work at the cafe, and had fallen head over heels with the boss's handsome son, Gregory.

"Do you think it's a good idea? I mean, does it not cause a lot of hurt knowing that you have no future with that person, that they have another life elsewhere which doesn't include you?" Nina continued.

"See, that's the beauty of summer romances. Right from the start you know where everyone stands and there are no expectations on either side."

"But what if expectations creep in anyway? Whether you like it or not?"

"Sometimes in life, it doesn't hurt to avoid overthinking things. Be like a leaf sometimes, just let the wind guide you. Refuse to be drawn into deep, negative thoughts that are sure to deter. So what if it hurts when the days of summer are gone and romance disappears? You'll have the memories to keep you going until the next one," she added with a wink.

Then looked at poor Nina's deeply troubled face.

Oh dear. She'd obviously fallen hard.

24

Back in the cottage, Grace was breathing heavily and close to cancelling the outing.

The boys were racing around yelling with joy about the prospect of going swimming, and she felt her insides clench.

She remembered her earlier thoughts. This was unnecessary, she told herself.

For starters, there was usually a lifeguard and secondly, the deep end would be a good way away from the shallow side.

Thirdly, she would be there, wouldn't she?

Her mind and heart were wired to her boys. Her instincts usually rose to the surface when one of them disappeared. She could trust herself.

Grace took several deep breaths, and plastered a smile on her face for the twin' sake.

She followed them into their bedroom, and stood against the door frame, watching them throw swimming trunks and towels into their bags haphazardly.

"Can you please—?" she started to say, then stopped.

What was the harm if the towels were not perfectly folded? So what if the boys were now kicking the bags around like footballs? It was just harmless fun.

She watched them for a moment longer. "I'll be in my room, packing my stuff, OK?" she said, resisting the strong urge to admonish them.

She had never worn her new red swimming suit and she hoped that it would fit. But Grace was not overly worried about that. Her diet was pretty stable and she had weighed the same for as long as she could remember.

To her surprise, a twinge of excitement was growing from somewhere inside her, and she felt as the boys probably did—excited to be going somewhere different to do something fun.

If only she lived in a place like this, Grace thought as they walked towards the leisure centre on the other side of town, each boy holding one hand.

It was so pretty and relaxed, and people were so friendly that you immediately felt at home.

Lakeview looked like a town straight out of a picture postcard. Bright colours splashed the old buildings that lined both sides of the street.

The cafe was the centre of it all of course, and Grace gave a friendly wave to one of the waitresses wiping the tables outside. Nina, she recalled.

They walked further on; the leisure club was a little way out and she and her boys walked along the paved path, making their way inside.

How lovely it was to never have to use your car either.

Saying hello to the friendly Motiv8 receptionist, Grace paid and as soon as she let go of their hands, the boys were all over the place, never mind that it was their first time there.

She closed her eyes and counted to three, then caught up with them and grabbed both arms.

When they reached the door to the ladies' changing room, there were the usual protests when Josh noticed a picture of a female form on the door.

"I'm *not* changing in the girls' bathroom."

"You have no choice. We all have to change here," Grace said in a firm tone, hardly recognising it as her own.

Much to her surprise, Josh dropped his arms from his chest and followed her in.

She wanted to jump in glee. That small success boosted her confidence considerably, and for once she felt like a capable mum.

Surely she could handle whatever the boys unleashed next?

25

In the changing rooms, she looked at her reflection in the mirror. The swimming suit fitted her perfectly, moulding itself against her slim figure. She wished that Kevin was here to see her.

Well, his loss, Grace thought with a muffled giggle.

She folded the boys' clothes and they made their way out of the changing rooms.

Actually there was a shallow pool area, she noticed, her whole body relaxing.

The kids' section was charmingly laid out with a small yellow slide that stopped bang in the middle of the pool.

The boys went straight in while Grace gingerly put her feet in, and felt like a giant with the water reaching well below her knees.

She slid down and sat on the tiled floor, enjoy the feeling of warm water swirling around her body.

There was no one yet in the kids pool, making it easier to watch the twins.

Jake approached the slide and tried to climb it from the wrong way round. He laughed when he couldn't manage more than a short distance and laughingly slid back into the pool. His brother followed suit.

Grace bit her tongue from telling them to do it the right way. There were no other kids here, so there was no harm in what the boys were doing, she chided herself.

She even found herself laughing at their antics.

Kids were so creative in their games, she thought watching them lazily.

Josh was trying to push his brother further up the slide, but still not managing to push him far up.

Giving up, they came out of the pool of their own accord and went round to climb the slide in the proper way.

Grace laughed at the splash made when each boy slid into the water.

Twenty or so minutes later, she watched a woman come towards the kids' pool holding a little boy's hand. He looked to be about the same age as her twins.

She wore a white swimming suit that showed off her hour glass figure. Grace thought she looked out of place in these surroundings; she belonged on the cover of a magazine. With her long glossy hair and sunglasses pushed on her forehead, she looked every inch a model.

"Mum I want to use the slide," the boy said, confirming that the woman was his mother.

"OK, Mikey go on," she said, and came towards where Grace sat on the edge.

Grace duly smiled at her and the woman smiled back. She too slid in to the water and sat next to her.

"I'm Emma," she said, extending a slim hand. Her smile matched the rest of her looks. Her teeth were milk white and even, and when she smiled, a dimple appeared on her cheeks.

"Grace," She returned the greeting pleasantly.

"I've seen you at Ella's, I think," Emma continued, and Grace cringed, hoping that she hadn't seen her during those times when she had been at her wits' end. "Your boys are so sweet, sometimes I wish I'd had two, so Mikey would always have company."

Grace laughed. "Do you know, I've never looked at it like that. I always see them as double trouble, but you're right. They always play together; my job is mostly to supervise."

"What are their names?" Emma asked.

They chatted, exchanging information about each other, and sharing experiences of raising boys.

Emma was a single mother, but she had her family to help. She didn't mention anything about the boy's father, but Grace somehow got the sense that this was a sore subject.

She looked at her own life and despite Kevin not coming on holiday with them, Grace felt lucky.

He was such a hands-on dad, and was always around to play with the boys.

It was good to put things in perspective sometimes.

Time flew by, and all too soon it was time to go. They all changed out of their swimming suits and left the leisure complex together.

Grace hadn't had that much fun in a long time. Emma was witty and lively, and she laughed a lot.

As they walked down the street, she even confided in Grace about some famous writer in Lakeview to finish a novel that she was hoping to snag.

She laughed at Emma's descriptions about how so far her antics weren't working so well, finding it difficult to believe that any man could resist her new friend.

They headed together to the cafe for a bite, and even though it was busy, managed to get a table outside where the three boys could play on the swings as they waited for their food.

"They do the tastiest club sandwich here, try it," Emma urged.

"Hello there."

It was Nina, the cafe's friendly but brisk waitress. Grace smiled brightly back, hoping to make up for the times she had caused a furore at the café.

Nina took their order and when she left, Grace and Emma's conversation continued, as though there had been no interruption.

She found herself confiding in the other woman her plans to go back to education and get a job once the boys started school.

Later, as they waved goodbye to Emma and Mikey, Grace mused over what a difference it made to have someone to chat to.

The day had been fun for her too and the boys as well. When they got home, she washed them and put them in front of the TV. They seemed so tired that for once there were no arguments about what to watch.

Grace remembered what Ella had told her about keeping the kids busy.

It worked, she realised in wonder, looking at how drowsy they seemed. They had no more energy left.

She ruffled their hair and went to the kitchen to prepare a light dinner.

For once, she felt like a normal mother, and the tight knot that usually accompanied her everywhere was absent.

If only Kevin could have seen her today, Grace thought feeling like she'd just run a marathon.

26

Marianne woke up as the bright morning sunlight splashed across her face. She rubbed her eyes and stretched, stopping when her legs bumped into something in the bed.

Startled, she laughed at herself when she saw that it was Donal.

She glanced at the watch by the bedside table. It was nine already. How was it that he was still asleep? Was he sick or something?

For the week that they had been here, Donal woke up at six or thereabouts every day. Who did that on holiday?

But thanks to Ella, now she felt a little bit more understanding towards him.

Marianne turned and faced him, putting her hand round his waist. It felt good to be close. The last few days had been so full of tension they had avoided any physical contact.

Donal turned without speaking and drew her into his arms. She loved the way he smelt in the morning.

Musky and his skin so hot, almost as though he had a fever. Slowly, her hands explored his body, and he responded, searching her mouth with his.

Twenty minutes or so later, Marianne lay in his arms, the tension of the previous week evaporating.

She could feel herself drifting back to sleep when she felt him start to get up. She moved away and continued to doze, revelling in the comfort of the bed.

At least he had managed to linger a little today.

Baby steps…

Donal padded softly across the room, and in her mind's eye, she could see him pick up his trousers from the chair, and put them on, trying to make as little noise as possible.

When he left the room, Marianne's mind returned to Grace and her twins.

There was something about having children so dependent on you that made you feel useful and needed.

She imagined what her and Donal's child might

look like. Probably he would be a solemn little thing like his father.

Marianne smiled. She figured that her husband would make a great dad all the same.

Seeing him playing football that time with Grace's boys had brought out maternal urges in her like never before. She longed for a baby.

No, that wasn't quite correct. She had *moments* like now when she longed for a baby.

But watching Donal engrossed in his work life, buried in his computer and waking up in the early hours to issue instructions, she felt differently.

Having a baby now would be taking a risk. She didn't want to end up as one of those women who were always complaining about their husbands not being there to help raise the children.

Despite Ella's counsel, she still hadn't figured out what to do about their situation.

She decided to put it at the back of her mind and would ponder over it later.

Marianne turned torward the door to doze, and was immediately confronted by delicious smells coming from downstairs.

She frowned. The evidence was there, but she almost refused to believe it.

The last time Donal had made any sort of meal for

her was years ago. The best he did was to take her out for dinner once every couple of months, and even then, it was usually connected to his work in one way or another.

Intrigued, she slipped from bed and wore her dressing gown over her light nightdress.

She went to the adjoining bathroom first, washed her face and freshened up. Then followed the smell downstairs to the kitchen.

She stood against the doorway, and looking at Donal standing over the frying pan, intently turning slices of bacon, her heart melted.

"Hey," she said softly.

"Morning, breakfast my princess?" he asked with a slight bow, making Marianne giggle.

"I'd love some."

"Come then." Donal pulled out a chair with flourish. He tucked a napkin into her robe and put a plate in front of her.

Piled on it was bacon, toast and a boiled egg. Next, he poured out a cup of tea and another for himself.

When he settled down opposite her, Marianne ate her breakfast, all the while reversing her earlier views of her husband.

"I know I haven't been attentive over the last couple of days, and I'm sorry. Forgive me?" he said.

Marianne smiled. "I forgive you, especially if you do this every morning."

27

Donal's attention lasted until after breakfast, when he excused himself to answer a few emails.

Marianne showered and dressed, and two hours later, Donal was still hunched over his computer.

She left the house and walked aimlessly, until once again she found herself in front of the cafe.

Ella was having a coffee at one of the outside tables, and Marianne approached.

"Can I join you?" she asked, not wanting to sit alone.

Ella smiled brightly, as though it were the best offer she had had all day.

"I just wanted to say thank you for your advice. I

really needed someone to talk to that time," Marianne said.

Ella smiled. "You're welcome. We all have days when things get to be too much. Have you figured out a solution yet?"

Marianne shook her head. "No, I still have no idea what to do."

"Have you tried talking to him?"

"I have, a thousand times, but it's as if he doesn't hear a word I say. Or he changes for a couple of hours and then like a duty done, he reverts to his old behaviour. I'm at my wits end; I really don't know what to do now."

"Maybe you should just try and enjoy this time away by yourself a little? The town has a lot to offer, try and sample some of it. It would be a real shame for you to spend your time here feeling stressed about everything."

Marianne thought about it. She had read about Lakeview's famous hiking trails and the river rafting that took place in the nearby Wicklow Mountains.

She had seen TV programs of people river rafting, and the sport had always fascinated her.

She had mentioned it to Donal already, and he had mumbled in that vague way he had of speaking when his mind was on something else.

Ella had a point. What was stopping her from enjoying all this on her own?

"You can't be responsible for the actions of other people. Have fun, grab happiness where you can, life is very short. I'm sixty, and I can tell you those years have just gone by in a wink," Ella said.

"Do you know, that's exactly what I'll do. I've been trying to interest Donal in all the activities around here, but he doesn't seem remotely interested. I wanted to try the hiking trail, the one that goes up into the hills," Marianne said, her eyes lighting up with excitement.

"Why don't I ask Nina if she'd like to take you? She's brilliant at showing people round the trails."

"Oh, I don't want to be a bother."

"Nonsense, Nina loves hiking, she'll be delighted for the opportunity to show off her knowledge."

"Well, if you're sure, I'd be happy to have some company."

Suddenly the next few days did not look so dull.

A few minutes later Nina came out and said hello. They hadn't formally met, though Marianne had of course come across her in the cafe.

"Marianne wants to go hiking, but she doesn't know too many people around, so I thought you might like to take her up on the trail when you're free?"

Nina's face immediately brightened and she smiled widely. "It would be a pleasure. I'll probably enjoy the walk more than you do. Mind if my four year old comes too though? He's off school at the moment, and my right hand man."

"Of course not and thank you so much," Marianne said. "Both of you."

"You're very welcome. We love visitors around here, don't we Nina? Now would you like a cup of tea or some juice?"

"Tea would be great, thanks," Marianne said, suddenly feeling as if she was amongst old friends.

28

That same afternoon Nina was manning the cafe alone, while Ella caught up on bookkeeping.

Strangely the place was uncharacteristically quiet now, she thought as she made herself a cup of coffee. It happened like that sometimes, and then like an avalanche, a huge crowd would flood in.

She'd just got her coffee and sat down at a table near the counter when she heard footsteps behind her.

"Hi stranger!" Emma greeted. She sat down on the chair next to Nina's, commenting on how quiet the café was.

"I was just thinking that myself," she replied, trying to dissect her feelings.

She and Emma had been friends for a couple of years now. So why did she feel this ... dullness on seeing her today?

"Coffee?" she asked.

"Yes, I'd love a cup."

Nina stood up and returned with a fresh brew.

"So, I haven't seen Sam for a few days, not since we went rafting," Emma commented. "I wonder if he's OK?"

Nina looked up in surprise. "Of course he's OK, why wouldn't he be? Sometimes when he's caught up in his novel, he holes himself away in there for days."

"I wish he'd hole himself away with me for a couple of days," her friend replied with a gleam in her eye.

"Ah so you do have a crush on him," Nina said, deflated afresh. "I did wonder last week on the trail."

"He's a single guy - of course I have a crush on him. *And* he's a bit of a celebrity. The perfect catch." Then she giggled. "Ah, Sam's cute but not really my type, too quiet. Still, I'd never pass up a man with money."

Nina was aghast. She knew Emma could be shallow, but now she felt as though the person sitting next to her was a complete stranger.

Poor Sam. She hoped that he hadn't fallen hook line and sinker for Emma's recent flirtations.

For more reasons than one.

"So how did the rafting go?" she asked.

"It was fun. He enjoyed himself, which is the most important thing of course," Emma said. "He has this awards do in Dublin next week, and I'm hoping he'll invite me. I've been throwing strong hints but so far nothing."

"Oh," was all Nina could think of saying.

"Do you think you could put in a word for me, you know friend to friend?" she asked, flashing one of the persuasive smiles she was famous for.

"And how would I go about doing that?"

"Well, you could start by inserting into conversations what a great catch *I* am ....

Nina made a noise of agreement in reply and sipped at her coffee, whilst contemplating her friend's intentions.

She felt very confused at her own judgment. Had Emma always been this calculated? She had never really paid too much attention to her friend's love life or questioned her interest in a guy.

But wanting a man for what he could do for you was wrong. Or any other person for that matter.

Still, there was nothing that Nina could do, and in truth it was none of her business.

Sam was a grown-up who could sort out his own issues.

29

But as if on cue, the man himself pushed open the door of the café.

Sam walked in, looking like he had come straight from the shower. His hair was damp, some of it clinging to the back of his neck. The skin on his face was slightly pink, probably from the force of the water in the shower.

Just then Nina would have given anything to stroke that face and hold him, inhaling the scent of his masculine cologne.

"Hello ladies," he greeted, smiling.

"Hi there, stranger - we were just talking about you actually," Emma stood up and planted a light kiss right on Sam's lips, and Nina was interested to note how uncomfortable that seemed to make him.

He made a movement of shrinking away, and she was relieved to see that despite Emma's best efforts, he didn't seem to be particularly interested in her romantically.

"What can I get you?" she asked him.

"A coffee would be great. Could I have a takeaway club sandwich as well?"

"Of course. If you like, I can pack you something for later too," she said, guessing that he was planning to work long hours all day and would likely forget to eat.

"Nina, you're a gem," he grinned, leaning against the counter.

After a few minutes, she'd packed up Sam's order and saw him off. Then she went back to join her friend at the counter.

"What's up with him I wonder?" Emma said sulkily. "The other day we got along so well, now he's behaving as if we were siblings or something."

Nina hid her smile. Then she noticed a newspaper on the worktop that hadn't been there.

"Where did this come from?"

Emma's eyes widened with delight. "Must be Sam's. Perfect, just the excuse I need." She jumped from her chair.

Nina watched, exasperated afresh, as her friend

hurried out of the café and sashayed around the corner towards the cottages.

She waited a few minutes for her to return but to no avail. Ten minutes went by then twenty, and then finally Emma came back, looking mightily pleased with herself.

"He invited me to the awards thing! It's on Saturday night, so I'm thinking we should stay over in Dublin, make it a romantic getaway?" Emma grinned like the cat that got the cream. "You OK to take Mikey overnight for me?"

When Nina nodded mutely, her friend stood up. "Great. Gotta go, I'll talk to you later. Wasn't it pure luck that I came along when I did?" she added happily.

Yes, pure luck, she thought, trying to dampen down the ache she felt about Sam spending a romantic night away in Dublin with Emma.

Now, thinking back on the conversation she'd had with Ella, Nina felt like a complete idiot.

Somebody might be having a summer romance. But it definitely wasn't her.

30

When Nina grew up, she wanted to be Marianne Cohen. The woman was beautiful and stylish, with an enviable career and she seemed so well put together, so organised.

"Your husband didn't want to join us?" she asked when a day or so later she, Marianne and little Patrick set off on the hiking trail around the lake.

Marianne made a face. "Oh he's too caught up in his work to leave it for a few hours," she said, sounding completely unruffled that instead of touring Lakeview with her husband, she was doing it with a complete stranger.

"His loss then." Nina joked. "It's such a beautiful day today."

"His loss indeed. So where to first, Guide?"

Nina took her to up the hills to the meadow, and like most visitors (and Sam) Marianne exclaimed when she saw it.

"It's so beautiful. Oh, I wish Donal could see this." A sad look crossed over her pretty features, before she perked up again.

There and then, Nina knew that it was a front. Seemed like Marianne wasn't carefree as she seemed?

Feeling bad for her, and at the same time applauding her quietly for putting on a brave front, Nina vowed to make it a fun day.

It was ten in the morning, a good time to walk among the trees when the day was not so warm.

Nina reeled off bits of information about the meadow and the surrounding countryside in general.

They watched butterflies chase each other and suspend themselves over thin pieces of grass, while Patrick tried to chase them.

Her mind strayed again to Sam as it always did these days when she wasn't so busy. She had served him breakfast again yesterday morning, and in return, had gotten a smile that had brightened up the rest of her day.

More than just looks, he was kind and funny too.

"If this is a small sample of the Lakeview

surroundings, I'm moving here permanently," Marianne joked now.

"You're welcome to, the more the merrier."

"But really, it must be a wonderful place to raise children?" Marianne looked wistful.

"It is. Do you have kids yourself?" Nina asked, hesitant about intruding on the other woman's privacy.

"No, not yet, but I'd love to eventually," she replied, looking sad.

'Oh I'm sure you will," Nina reassured her cheerfully. "In the meantime, enjoy the time when it's all yours." She smiled at her little son who was racing happily around the meadow. "They're great, but they have this way of taking over your entire life."

"So I hear, but at this point, I think I might be ready for that."

"Perhaps next summer when you come back you'll have a little one in tow?" Nina teased.

That seemed to cheer Marianne up and she nodded happily.

They chatted easily as they walked through the woods, emerging from the other end of the trail and a golf course adjoined the wooded area, a green lush stretch of hilly and flat land.

It was an enjoyable morning for both women, which ended in a lunch at the café.

"What do I owe you for a wonderful tour?" Marianne asked Nina, her skin pink and glowing from being outdoors.

"Oh no, nothing at all. I enjoyed it too."

"You're really good at it, you know." Marianne said. "A natural. You should think about converting something like that from a hobby to a profession. That's how I started in the cosmetics industry. Make-up was a hobby for me, until I made it a career. You could too, you know."

Nina blushed at the avalanche of compliments.

"Thank you, maybe I'll give it some thought when Patrick is older."

"Meanwhile, lunch is on me. It's the least I can do after such a morning. It took my mind off things, and I needed that."

"You're welcome. Thanks for the lunch; I'll take you up on that - I'm famished. " Nina glanced at her watch.

She still had an hour or so left before her evening shift started. Enough time to take little Patrick to his grandfather's house and get back again to the cafe.

She followed Marianne to a table in the centre, while little Patrick went to play in the kids' corner.

Ella came to take their order, beaming at them and slid into the empty third chair.

"How was it?" she asked turning to Marianne.

"It was great, just what the doctor ordered. I'm even feeling brave enough to try river rafting one of these days."

"That's great. I told you this town has a lot to offer. I'm glad you got to sample some of it instead of staying cooped up in your cottage."

Nina was puzzled, why didn't Marianne get out more often?

Her attention wandered from Ella and Marianne's conversation, when out of the window she spied Sam headed in this direction.

Man, he was handsome. From where she sat, Nina could observe him coming in covertly without the fear that he would see her.

By now she knew his favourite table, which was by the window. He paused for a moment at the door, his eyes roamed round the café and then he continued walking to his table.

Their eyes met, and Nina waved, and just that moment, a dark haired man walked in behind Sam, wielding his phone like it was a weapon.

31

He looked around the café, and his eyes stopped at their table.

"There you are; you've been gone forever!" he moaned to Marianne. "I was wondering if you were going to come back at all."

Ah, the elusive husband, Nina thought understanding, as the other woman went to make introductions.

"Nina, this is my husband Donal, and honey, this is Nina, the lovely lady I told you was giving me a tour of the hills this morning. And of course you know Ella," Marianne said, her voice cold.

Donal looked terse. "I told you I wanted to come too."

Marianne rolled her eyes. "You were on the phone

when I was getting ready and I told you I was going, but you never paid me any heed. We had a great time anyway. The trail is gorgeous."

Ella quickly excused herself, as did Nina while Donal slid into the chair that Nina vacated.

She could hear their angry voices exchange harsh words.

Now she knew Marianne's issue. She and her husband were here on holiday, yet he was too busy to enjoy the time with his wife.

She soon forgot about the warring couple though, as she approached Sam's table.

"Can I join you? I'm a paying customer for a change today," she said, and got a huge smile in response.

"Of course." He quickly stood up and pulled the chair back for her. Nina loved the gentlemanly gesture and she smiled back in gratitude.

When he sat back down, she saw that he had a stubble of a moustache above his upper lip, and felt like running her finger across it.

"So how was the river rafting with Emma that time?" she asked, saying the first thing that popped into her brain.

"It was OK; I'd think I'd have enjoyed it much

more if you took me. Though it seems you only give personalised tours to special people?" he teased.

Nina's breath caught, and she told herself to act cool. She smiled and tossed her hair behind her head, vaguely aware that now she was acting like a teenager.

Was he flirting with her?

"Well, I do and you're half-right, I only give tours to people I like," she joked back.

Sam's face fell and he feigned deep hurt. "I take it that I'm not among that group of very lucky people?"

He is flirting. Nina's brain almost stopped functioning.

"You could be, but then I also dislike competition," she went on, her tone more serious than she'd intended.

"What competition?" Sam said. "Go on, take me hiking then. Or anything else you prefer. Take this lonely writer out on a date."

Nina contemplated him and saw that he was serious.

Her heart did somersaults and she wanted to shriek *yes of course*, in response.

But her naturally cautious nature took over.

"You're seeing Emma though, aren't you?" she murmured softly.

Sam looked taken aback. "Emma? Your friend Emma? What makes you think that?"

Nina kept quiet.

"Believe me, Emma's not interested in me, nor I in her. I know she's your friend, but I'll tell you anyway. She just enjoys being seen with me because I'm a micro-celebrity. I know that. Nothing to do with me as a person."

Nina was stunned. He knew?

"So what do you think, how about a proper outing, just you and me?" he repeated.

Smiling shyly, Nina nodded. She would love to go hiking with Sam.

Or anywhere.

32

"You should have waited for me," Donal complained, as he and Marianne walked back to the cottage after a tension-filled meal at the cafe.

She ignored him and walked on. Nothing could spoil her good mood. She knew Donal, and the fact that she had gone out alone wasn't the issue. Then her mind returned to Nina and she froze.

"Oh no!" Marianne said her hand flying to her mouth. "I was supposed to buy Nina lunch and I completely forgot about it. Let me go back and apologise."

"She'll understand, you can explain another time," Donal said, looking impatient.

Marianne felt awful. Nina would think her so

ungrateful. They had spent such a wonderful morning together. She was a good person to be around. She knew everything there was to know about Lakeview. And she was so kind to take her out.

She turned her attention back to Donal. Every few seconds he ran a hand through his hair, as if it were a comb. Something was on his mind. He would tell her when he was ready.

Meanwhile she tried to recreate that heady feeling at the top of the trail that morning. It had felt like she was floating on air.

"You're smiling?" Donal said, almost accusingly.

"Yes I am." Marianne said turning to him with a wide grin. "I feel happy. There's something about the air in these parts that lifts your spirit. I feel as though I can do anything."

"Let's not go home just yet. Can we go for a walk?"

"Sure, anywhere in particular?"

"No, let's just walk on."

There passed the other cottages as they ambled further along the lakeside, and Marianne imagined the lives of the people inside.

Were they content, happy or sad? She felt like she had been at a crossroads for a long time, but she felt freer now.

She felt powerful; her destiny or future happiness

did not depend on one person. It was up to her, and that knowledge made her feel as though the world was hers for the taking.

Donal cleared his throat and she brought her attention back to him.

All along the water, there were park benches placed in strategic places, and now he held her hand and guided her to one. It was shaded by towering trees.

"I really thought you were gone," he said suddenly.

"I was gone," she replied idly. "Gone hiking with Nina."

He was quiet, as though trying to decide whether to continue with the conversation.

When he spoke again, his voice sounded so different, that if Marianne was not seating next to him, she would have sworn it belonged to another person.

It was raw and rugged. "I mean, thought you had left me."

33

He sounded so bereft, that Marianne immediately wanted to take him into her arms and comfort him.

"Why would you think that?" she asked incredulously.

He looked away into the distance.

"I realised what a eejit I've been, obsessed with my work and not paying you any attention. I told myself that if you'd left me I deserved it, but if you haven't, I'll do everything in my power to make you happy again," he said his eyes moist.

He looked at her and waited. Marianne wanted to cry. She had longed to hear those words for so long that when they came, she had no response.

"What happened to us lately, love?" she asked, her voice shaky.

"I don't know, but please tell me it's not too late."

"It's not too late. How could it be? I love you."

Donal moved closer and cupped her face in both his hands. "Not as much as I love you. You brighten my world. Without you, all these things we have, holidays, cars, promotions, they mean nothing, Marianne. You're my everything."

He pulled her into his arms and the floodgates broke. She sobbed into his chest, relief washing over her at the knowledge that Donal truly loved her.

When her sobs subsided, he gently wiped off the tears with the back of his hand.

They looked at each other and smiled shyly.

"I've been thinking, no more work for me in the remaining days of our time here. And when we go back home, I'll be leaving my work behind in the office. I don't want to lose you, or us."

"You don't know how happy that makes me feel," Marianne said. Then she cleared her throat, feeling that the time was right. "Do you remember that day at the park with Grace's boys?" she continued.

Donal nodded.

"You were so great with them. You'd make a wonderful father. What would you think about us starting a family?" she finished, and held her breath. "Not immediately of course," she added. "Once we've settled back down at home."

"Maybe," Donal said, his face blank. "Let me be honest though, honey. Kids scare the living daylights out of me. A human being dependent on you for everything. I feel as though we need to build a solid financial base before thinking of kids."

Pragmatic as always, she thought fondly.

"It *is* a scary thought, but look at it this way. We own our own home, we have great jobs, and really we are better off than so many other people."

"College though?" Donal said, worry lines crisscrossing his forehead.

Marianne looked at him, and broke into laughter. She couldn't stop laughing, until tears rolled down her cheeks.

"What's funny?" he asked, setting her off again.

When she stopped, she turned to him. "Listen to yourself. You're worried about college fees for a child who has not even yet been conceived!" She stopped talking to wipe off her cheeks.

A tentative ghost of a smile appeared on Donal's face.

He grinned sheepishly. "OK, but you have to admit a kid is a lot of work. Look at poor Grace. She looks perpetually confused and harassed every time I see her."

"True, but there are other mothers with five kids in tow who look perpetually calm," Marianne pointed out.

He turned to her shocked. "You want *five* kids?"

She laughed. "Of course not, maybe two. And you?"

"One."

"Let's start with that and we can work from there," Marianne agreed, smiling.

"Right so, let's go back to the cottage and get started," Donal said wickedly, pulling her to her feet.

34

Nina continued with her lunch, watching the detail of Sam's face when he wasn't looking at her.

His dark eyes resembled her ex-boyfriend and Patrick's dad's Steve's a little; perhaps that had captured her attention that first day?

They turned dark when Sam was upset or disturbed, and she had seen him in both moods when his novel was not going well.

"How's your writing going?" she asked, quickly putting any comparisons with her ex out of her mind.

"Not so good, I've hit a bit of a hitch, but it'll work itself out," he replied, and then looked at her expectantly as though waiting for her to say something.

"What?" she asked.

"I'm waiting for the inevitable follow-up question, the one everybody asks."

"I'm not everyone and I have no further questions." Nina said, in a mock courtroom tone.

He laughed, and then mimicking a shrill voice said. "What's it about?"

Nina laughed. "You don't like being asked that?"

"No," Sam said. "In fact, the fastest way to kill your novel even before you start it is to talk about it. Thank you for never asking me that."

"You're welcome," By now she was glowing from the compliments. "Actually the truth is, I wouldn't want to know because it'll spoil my enjoyment when reading it. So you see, it's entirely selfish."

"You're a reader then? What kind of books do you like?" Sam asked.

"Of course I am. My favourite authors are Jane Austen, Maeve Binchy—"

The minutes passed by in a flash. When it was time to drop off little Patrick in time for her next shift, Nina stood up regretfully.

She would have loved for the lunch with Sam to stretch on. He was terrific company, and he made her laugh.

"That was good fun, thanks," she said.

Sam stood up. "I'm the one who should say thanks.

My morning had been unproductive, but now I feel completely re-energised. You're wonderful company Nina. You'll tell me when you are free again so we can go do something?"

She nodded, and with a wave and a bounce in her step, grabbed Patrick, and headed for her father's house.

The grin remained on her face all that evening until Ella commented on it and teased her a little.

She was just so relieved that Sam and Emma had nothing between them.

Now the thought of spending time alone with him made her senses come alive. She remembered the way the hair on his arms stood and how much she would have loved to run her hand along his skin.

Slightly shocked at the direction her thoughts were taking, Nina cautioned herself.

A summer romance was one thing, but any thought of anything more was a recipe for disaster.

For one, she would be exposing herself to hurt.

She remembered what Ella had told her. The key was keeping things in perspective.

If something happened between her and Sam, and Nina desperately hoped it would, she must guard her heart and view it for what just it was, a brief summer romance.

35

The day after, Nina was waiting tables, her mind far away and a smile on her face. She felt giddy with excitement.

Yesterday before her shift ended, Sam had popped back to the cafe and officially invited her out.

A part of her was excited, but another was terrified.

The biggest question was, what if it didn't work between them? But that was silly. They had so much chemistry that you could cut it with a knife.

This would be the craziest, maddest thing she had ever done. A summer fling - imagine?

She made her way to the counter where Ella was standing, watching her speculatively.

"You've really fallen for him, haven't you?" she

said, tilting Nina's chin so that she could look into her eyes. "I'm so happy for you pet; you deserve every happiness and excitement."

"He's wonderful. I can't wait for tonight," she said, before her hands flew to cover her mouth when she realised what she had said.

"Oh, something big happening tonight?" Ella raised an eyebrow.

"Not really, he's just invited me for dinner at the cottage," she said, taking care to keep her eyes focused on anywhere else but on Ella. "Patrick's staying the night at Dad's."

"Hmm, be careful though, won't you?" the older woman said then, her voice laced with concern.

"I'm a big girl, I'll be fine," Nina said with more confidence than she felt.

"You may be, but pet, Sam has a lot more experience with these things than you do. For him it could well be just a summer fling. Don't fall in love with him, or is it already too late?" She gently touched Nina's shoulder.

"I promise I'll be careful. And don't worry, I know that Sam is a famous author, and probably has women throwing themselves at his feet all the time. I also know that right now the last thing I need is a relationship, not that there's an offer."

They both laughed.

"Ah, I think I just want to have some fun; you remember what it felt like to have someone, even if it's just temporary?"

"Of course I do," Ella said. "Enjoy yourself. I wish I had some pointers to offer, but I wouldn't remember, I'm too old for that kind of thing."

"I'm sure Joseph would disagree," Nina winked, as her boss went in the direction of her office.

She had lied though. Of course for her, this was way more than a summer romance. She had indeed fallen for Sam.

She felt excited and at peace when he was with her. But she was determined not to show him that, or else he would go off running.

The last thing someone like Sam wanted was a clingy woman. He too wanted to enjoy a summer fling with no strings attached.

Nina was prepared for that.

When the remaining time on his lease was over, they would go their separate ways.

End of story.

36

*E*vening came, and Nina quickly changed out of her work clothes.

Ella gave her a wink as she hurried out and she winked back, feeling odd, as though everyone could tell what she was planning for the evening.

She rushed up the main street and headed back to her little flat, not stopping to exchange pleasantries with the locals as she often did.

She felt clammy after the long day at work, and she longed to stand under a cool shower and wash off the grime from her skin.

In the privacy of her bedroom, Nina stripped and walked naked to the adjoining shower. She stood under the cool water letting it wash over her, her face turned upwards.

Then she poured a dollop of shower gel into her palm and rubbed it all over her body. Her mind was blank, concentrating in the simple pleasure of showering.

When she finished and turned off the water, Nina experienced a moment of panic.

Was she ready for this?

What if she froze, it had been so long since she'd been with a guy ... Then maybe she was running away with herself. Maybe Sam wouldn't make any kind of move at all ...

But if the chemistry between them was anything to go by, Nina knew chances were they would end up in each other's arms.

Her hair had always been easy to blow dry. In five minutes it was done and from her reflection in the mirror, she could tell it looked sleek and shiny.

It was a warm evening, and she chose a strapless lavender dress to wear for dinner and applied very little makeup, just a pale pink lip gloss and eye shadow.

The final touch was a dab of perfume on each wrist and on her neck.

When she was ready, she went to check the time on the clock in the kitchen. It was almost eight o'clock. Time to go.

Reaching Sam's cottage, she stood outside, frowning. The curtains were drawn and there was no sign of any activity inside.

Nina blinked. It actually looked dark inside. She would find out soon enough.

She knocked gently on the door, and a second later it swung open.

"My, aren't you a sight for sore eyes. You look ravishing." Sam said, his eyes running from her head to her toes.

"Thank you, you don't look too shabby yourself."

Sam had dressed up for the occasion. He wore a white shirt, tucked into khaki trousers. He looked smartly casual and Nina was glad that he had made the effort. He moved aside and let her in.

She knew these cottages well, but right then she barely recognised the place. It was lit by candles and the dining table had been converted into a table for two.

"It's beautiful!" she exclaimed.

"This way madame," Sam said, leading Nina to the dining table and pulling out a chair for her.

It was an open plan kitchen, and she watched him as he served dinner on two plates and then bring them to the table.

He sat down, and busied himself opening a bottle

of white wine. He looked up momentarily from his task and their eyes met. Nina hastily looked away concentrating on the food before her.

"I'm impressed." she said. "I didn't figure you for a cook."

"I have quite a few hidden talents." Sam said, catching her eye again.

37

Nina knew that her face was pink. She smiled shyly at the innuendo, and then moved the conversation back to food.

"I recognise pasta, but what's the rest of it?" she asked.

"It's lemon garlic penne. You can't go wrong with penne," Sam said with a grin.

She laughed. "Very smart. It smells wonderful."

"Dig in."

Nina hardly tasted the food, her mind full with Sam's presence. He had a way of filling up a room so that you were constantly aware of him.

"It's really tasty, thank you."

"Anything for you." He reached across the table

and touched her cheek. Nina was still, revelling in the feel of his strong hand brushing against her skin.

He ran his hand all the way to her lips then took it back.

"You had something on your cheek," he said, his eyes twinkling with mischief.

"A piece of pasta?"

Sam nodded furiously. "Yes, that's it."

They exchanged light banter during dinner, and oscillated between serious conversation and flirting.

"Have you thought any more about that tourist guide training?" he asked, as he brought dessert to the table.

Nina ignored his question and exclaimed over the dessert. It looked very familiar.

"Before you ask, yes it's Colm's Twix cake and I got it from the cafe. I should have known you'd recognise it immediately."

"It's OK, I love Twix cake."

Besides, Nina thought to herself, it would kill off the garlic taste in her mouth from the lemon pasta.

"I'm still waiting for your answer," Sam said, looking at her with his dark eyes and her heart skipped another beat. "Tour guide training?"

"Oh. I've been so busy that I haven't given it further thought," Nina said, knowing she was lying.

Other than Sam, she had thought of little else. She knew that by not thinking about going back to work proper when Patrick was in school that she was being a coward, and that was not who she was.

If she put her mind to it, she could do it.

"You're lying," Sam said.

"I am too," Nina confirmed with a laugh, "The truth is that I'm still thinking about it."

"Don't think too much, just do it," he said, and Nina thought that this could be applied to more than just her future career.

"Yes sir."

They finished dessert, and she was surprised when Sam walked to the stereo and put on some music.

He chose a soft ballad, and he came back and took her hand.

Happily, Nina stood up and was enclosed in his arms. He was taller than her by two inches or so, her head coming to his shoulder.

After a little while, as their bodies swayed to the music in perfect sync, their gazes met and when Sam slowly lowered his face to hers, everything faded to the background.

. . .

It was morning, Nina could tell even before she opened her eyes.

The atmosphere had changed, and already she could feel the warmth of the sun on her eyes. She thought about how the night with Sam had ended.

'What are you smiling at?" a gravelly voice said then.

Her eyes flashed open. Sam was propped up on his hand, looking adoringly at her.

"I thought you were still asleep," she accused.

"How can I sleep and miss watching *you* pretend to sleep," he said and kissed her forehead.

She burrowed herself happily into his chest and arms. She had missed the touch of a man, and so much else, she thought.

It had been over five years since she'd broken up with Patrick's father.

A fling, she reminded herself, as once again she relished the feeling of being in Sam's arms. These things happened the world over between people thrown together for short periods.

Just a summer fling, Nina repeated again in her head like a mantra, willing herself not to wish for anything more.

38

The town had obviously worked its magic again, Ella mused as she spied the couple at the corner table holding hands.

Nowadays Marianne and Donal only had eyes for each other. And this was the same couple who had spent most of their stay exchanging harsh words.

She was glad to see that they seemed to have worked out their problems.

She was manning the fort by herself today, since Nina was off. She picked up a cloth and wiped down a table that had just been vacated.

"Ella?" a voice called out.

It was Marianne, now alone at the table. From the corner of her eye, Ella saw Donal disappear towards the bathroom.

"Good to see you two looking so happy," she remarked.

"I just wanted to say thanks. The time here has been amazing for us," Marianne said. "Talking with you opened up my eyes to a lot of things. It was my fault as much as Donal's that our marriage was faltering."

"I'm just happy I could help - its reward enough to see the two of you acting like newlyweds."

Then Ella made herself scarce when she spied Donal returning.

She then headed out to the outdoor seating area to check on Grace and the twins, who were enjoying a snack.

"Are ye OK? Do you need anything?" she asked.

Much to her surprise, today the boys were seating down and quietly eating their cookies and milk.

"We're great thanks," Grace smiled.

Ella looked at her closely. Something was different about her lately. Then it hit her.

The nervousness and anxiety she usually wore like a cloak were gone. Grace looked peaceful as she sipped at her tea.

"May I join you for a second?" Ella asked.

"Of course."

"What did you do to them?" she said gesturing at the twins. "They like little angels now."

Grace laughed. "Nothing, I think they're just tired. I can't swim you see, so I thought while I was here I might as well enrol myself for swimming lessons down at the leisure centre. The boys aren't great swimmers either so we've all been taking lessons together. We've spent every afternoon this week at the pool at Motiv8, that's why they're so wrecked."

"Wow," Ella smiled, looking at the boys again.

"I know - lessons have kept us pretty busy," Grace said. "Nicola's a tough taskmaster."

"Nicola's teaching you?" Ella said, smiling. "She's the best."

"She's been brilliant, and I must admit I was a bit sceptical at first..." Grace said conspiratorially, and Ella smiled.

Outsiders often felt that way about Motiv8's manager, completely underestimating her abilities, but once they got to know her, very quickly changed their minds.

She was a force of nature and Ella was especially glad Nicola seemed to have taken Grace under her wing.

No better woman.

"Tomorrow is our last day, believe it or not," Grace

said wistfully. "I'd have loved to stay on a bit longer but we'd only booked the cottage for two weeks."

"We'll miss having your around. Will you come back next summer maybe?"

"Most definitely. I appreciate all your help too, Ella. In my time here, and especially after our conversation, I've come to look at the boys as a joy instead of a burden. And since I've done that, I realise they're actually good fun."

Ella beamed in reply and then headed back inside, whistling softly to herself.

Yet another example of Lakeview's magic.

39

When they'd paid their bill, Grace shepherded the twins out of the café, and back towards their cottage.

The food had perked them up and they skipped along as they walked.

"Keep to the walking path, guys," she chided mildly.

They strolled along, enjoying watching people pass by, wearing sun hats and colourful summer clothes.

To Grace, it was as though someone had poured a bucketful of rainbow paint over Lakeview this last week.

She thought back to her conversation with Kevin the night before. As expected, work was so crazy her husband had never managed to make it down at weekends, and he couldn't wait for their return home.

This stay had been such a godsend actually and she felt like a totally different person from the one who had first arrived two weeks ago.

Grace had made some friends too, but most importantly she had learned to relax.

The last week in particular had been a revelation.

Before, she had seen her boys as two annoying little burdens, determined to make her own life as difficult and as stressful as they could.

Now she laughed softly. Kevin was right all along. They were just kids being kids.

And she had learned a new trick too. Whenever one of the boys spoke to her, she listened attentively without interrupting and then gave whatever it was serious consideration. She had noticed that by doing that, they were learning to trust her.

She couldn't wait to go back home now, back to Kevin and her regular life.

Although there would also be some changes.

For one, Grace was determined more than ever to go back to college and get her Masters, and then look for a job.

Regretfully she figured it was also time to let go of Marie. She knew she had come to rely too much upon the nanny - had used her as a crutch of sorts - and now that the boys were older they no longer needed full time care.

Grace also wanted to spend as much time as possible with them before they went to school.

She felt as though she had already missed out so much of their formative years, and had a lot to make up for.

They would continue with swimming lessons together too. The biggest problem Grace thought, was how to disengage herself from her mummy friends.

They were nice people, but there was no doubt that the group had major competitive issues.

Every mum wanted to be the one who took their child to the most classes and activities, who took the best approach at raising them, wanted to be the expert at motherhood.

Sure it was OK to sign them up for stuff, but being alone with the boys had taught Grace that it might well be the parents, not the kids who needed all this activity?

Kids just needed to spend time with their parents.

No longer a chore, now she saw time spent with them as an opportunity to bond.

Wow, Kevin would think someone else had taken

his wife and put a clone in her place! she thought with a chuckle.

Next summer she would make sure they would all make it down to Lakeview. But privately she was glad that this time Kevin hadn't come along, and she'd finally had the chance to find her feet with the boys in her own way and in her own time.

They walked on until they reached their cottage. "Time to pack up for tomorrow boys," Grace said.

"Please let's stay longer. I like it here with you Mummy, it's so much fun," Josh said.

"Yes, let's stay forever Mummy," Jake added pleadingly.

Grace's eyes filled with tears. No other words had ever sounded as sweeter.

"It was fun being here with you too," she finally said. "But Daddy misses us."

She wiped the tears away before the boys saw them, and led them upstairs, her heart expanding by the second as the words from the boys - her sons - kept repeating themselves in her brain.

Mummy.

For the first time in her life, Grace felt like she'd finally lived up to the word.

40

In the final days of summer, the café was not as busy as it had been for the previous three months.

Nina served a few customers in the morning, but now it was eleven and the place was almost empty.

The last few days she had not seen much of Sam, though he popped in regularly for a quick breakfast and a stolen kiss if the opportunity allowed.

But for the remainder of his stay, he was kept busy with his novel. He'd told her that she had opened up the pores of his creativity and his mind was overflowing with ideas for his novel.

Nina was happy for him, but she missed spending long hours with him, being together or just holding each other.

Today, a cloud of sadness was hovering.

The last few days in particular had given her an inkling of how hard it would be when he went back to Dublin.

She felt an emptiness that hadn't existed before. It was easy to think that you could keep everything in perspective and she wondered how other people handled summer romances.

Already she could tell that she wasn't handling hers very well. She wanted Sam to be with her forever.

Yet he had his own life. He was a successful author who had responsibilities. But more than that, he was probably only physically attracted to her.

When they were together, he never gave an inkling to what his thoughts were. He never said what he felt about her, and so Nina also took her cue from him and never said anything either.

They were just two people out to have fun together weren't they?

A familiar figure walking down the street caught her attention. It was Emma, her hair bouncing as she walked. You would think that she was going somewhere fancy by the way she was dressed.

But that was Emma's way, Nina thought fondly, happy that any previous resentment she'd felt toward her friend had disappeared.

Emma pushed the door open and walked in.

"Hi, good to see you, where have you been lately, busy-bee?" Nina greeted.

"I've been around, actually," her friend said, then leaning forward conspiratorially added, "and I've got news."

"Don't keep me in suspense, tell!"

"Well, I met someone ... over at the golf course."

Nina's eyes widened. Emma was fast; she attracted men like bees to flowers.

"His name is Chris and he's a property developer. He owns a chain of hotels all over the world, and guess what? He wants us to go exclusive," Emma finished her eyes twinkling. "I'm not sure if I know how to do that."

Nina laughed. "Is he kind?"

She contemplated the question, and then nodded. "He is, kind and sweet, which of course also means a bit boring. But he and Mikey are getting along great. He's teaching him how to play golf."

"Hold on to that one then. Men who are good with kids are a rare find," Nina said, thinking of Sam who was brilliant with Patrick.

"I know. Did I mention that he's rich too?" Emma said and both women laughed. "So any news with you?"

Nina wondered whether to tell her about Sam. She thought of the way Emma had just confided in her without any reservations and decided to go for it.

"Actually ..." Nina said coyly.

"You're blushing!" Emma banged the table. "You're seeing someone too? Who? Do I know him?"

"Stop being dramatic, we're not telling everyone here," Nina said, looking around. "And yes, you do sort of know him. Sam."

Emma's eyes widened like saucers. "Sam the author? You snagged that cold human being who wouldn't give me the time of day?"

Nina laughed at her friend's expression. "He's sweet and kind and very thoughtful."

Emma squinted. "Are we talking about the same person?"

And she was off, making Nina laugh with her antics. From the description that Emma gave, it was clear that this new guy was a good match for her.

They spoke for a while longer and when her friend left, Nina's spirits were a little higher.

So what if this was a summer romance? She would hurt for a few weeks, but she would never forget Sam.

With that she whistled as she went about her work.

"What are you so happy about?" Ella said to her

when they found themselves alone behind the counter.

"Nothing in particular." Nina said. "I'm just happy."

"Lucky you."

At her tone, Nina looked at her employer and friend in surprise. "What's wrong, it's not like you to be so down in the dumps."

"I hate the end of summer, it makes me feel so maudlin. The change is too drastic. I love the way Lakeview is full of activities and people. I hate autumn," Ella groaned, making Nina burst out laughing.

She pulled her into a quick hug. "Summer will be back sooner than you know. Besides we have winter to look forward to now. Maybe another famous Christmas party?"

"After all the drama last time," Ella said wryly, "I'm not sure my heart could take it.'

41

That evening, Sam popped over to Nina's for dinner.

She had made a casserole and salad, and Sam brought a bottle of wine.

It was awkward with Patrick there because they had to keep their feelings for each other hidden.

Whatever was going on between them was theirs alone, and Nina did not want her five-year old privy to that part of her life.

The day she introduced someone as her boyfriend to her son, it would be a serious relationship, she mused, serving chunks of the casserole.

"So what are we celebrating?" she asked Sam afterwards, when Patrick went to watch TV and they remained at the table.

"Can we not have nice wine when there's nothing to celebrate?"

"We can, but something tells me there's more to it than that."

"You're right, there is. I finished my first draft today," he said beaming.

"Oh wow, that's brilliant. Congratulations."

Though a moment later, the implications of his finishing his novel hit her, and Nina grew solemn.

Now, he had no reason to remain in Lakeview, did he?

He would soon leave and return to his exciting life in Dublin. She felt bereft as though he had already left, and she felt his touch when he lifted up her chin to look at her eyes.

"What is it? You look so sad."

Nina plastered a smile onto her face. "Nothing, I'm grand."

"You're not a very good liar you know," he said. "It'll be hard for me too. You and this place has become so special to me."

She smiled at his attempts to cheer her up. "Ah, we lead such different lives," she said.

Sam looked puzzled. "How so?"

"Well, you have this amazing life as a famous author, jetting from one awards do to the other. Going on book tours to exotic locations. For us here, life is fairly quiet. Lakeview is lovely, but hardly the most glamorous of places."

Sam looked at her, astounded. And then to Nina's surprise, he burst into laughter.

"Is that how you envision my life? You couldn't be further from the truth. I live alone in the city at a house way too large for me. I don't have a cat or a dog, I dislike pets. I wish I could take you and Patrick back with me."

Her heart beat hard.

"But I can't ask you to do that. I can't uproot you and your son from your home - and leave your dad, I know that," Sam continued, and shook his head. "It's true what they say about people not appreciating their surroundings. The time I've spent here has been wonderful. You're so lucky to live in this town, Nina. You all know each other; it's like one big happy family."

"I suppose we are."

"Where I live, I don't even know who my neighbour is. I wake up, write for a couple of hours, then respond to emails and return calls. Most afternoons, I'm out in the garden or on the sofa reading a novel—my reward for the morning's work. As for the awards dos and books tours, they're not as exciting anymore. I've done them for so many years."

"So when are you leaving?" Nina said.

Sam looked at her for a moment. "Tomorrow."

She gasped. "So soon?"

"I have to. My publishers have been waiting for this book for a *long time*. I need to go home and go over it with my agent and talk to my editor. There's not much time remaining between now and the publication date. Not to mention that the lease on the cottage is up anyway."

Looking at him and hearing the excitement in his voice as he spoke about his book, Nina realised that for Sam, summer was indeed well and truly over, and so was their affair.

She envied him for his ability to move on so quickly and to remain detached. She thought back to Ella's words of warning.

He was used to this kind of thing.

She forced a smile and promised that she would not act needy. "I'm so happy for you," she said.

"Thanks. For a while there, I really thought I'd lost my mojo," Sam said. "I'm going to head off in the afternoon, give us a chance to have a few last moments together tomorrow morning before I go?"

"Sure." While she appreciated the gesture, she could see that already his mind was back in Dublin.

Nina had no choice but to come to terms with the fact that this time tomorrow, the man she'd fallen in love with would be too.

42

A couple of leaves slid down from the patio parasol as Nina snapped it shut. Today was the official last day of summer. The kids were back at school tomorrow.

Sam had been gone for two weeks, and still the deep hole of emptiness lingered.

She hated walking around with a long face, even Ella had commented on it. Nina, who loved all the seasons was feeling weighed down by the thought of the approaching autumn.

She missed Sam with a fierceness that surprised her. He had filled her life with such excitement and affection and worst of all ... hope.

She closed the last parasol and stood there, lost in thought.

"It'll get better you know, and you'll have all those nice memories in the meantime," Ella said making Nina jump.

"I didn't hear you coming."

'I know. You look so sad and lost, love. Have you forgotten what we talked about before? About keeping things in perspective?"

"Easier said than done."

"Trust me, you'll be all right with time." Ella patted her on the shoulder and returned inside.

Nina looked at herself as her boss and friend might, and suddenly felt ashamed of herself.

She was behaving like a lovesick teenager, which would not help matters at all.

She threw her shoulders back and made a resolution to move on.

Especially when Sam had not as much as called her once since he left.

So why should she spend her valuable time crying over a man who had clearly moved on?

Nina decided that her first line of business when she left work today was to go home and browse the internet for tourism educational courses.

Now that Patrick was starting school, she needed something else to focus on. Why not pursue something that everyone seemed to think she was so good at?

Despite her melancholy, at this decision, Nina felt something akin to excitement.

43

Soon, autumn had well and truly made its appearance, and Ella shuddered at the biting cold and rain that she knew was just round the corner.

Paddy Collins had stopped coming for breakfast, but she knew they would see him next summer when he ventured out again.

She thought about the summer tourists who had come to Lakeview this year with more than one kind of baggage.

Grace and her boys; Ella hoped that the young mum had managed to hold on to that sense of peace she had gotten from her stay here.

Would she ever see her and her boisterous twins

again? It was difficult to tell. When the summer visitors left, they were always so sure of their return, but until you saw them again, there was no way of knowing.

The person that Ella felt sure would return though, was Marianne.

She chuckled as she remembered how she and her husband had been in the last few days of their holiday. Like new lovers, holding hands at every opportunity.

Ella knew that some people managed to hold on to that chemistry for all of their lives. Perhaps it would be the same for Marianne and Donal.

They would come for their summer break in Lakeview even when their hairs were greying.

That would be lovely.

Something had changed in Nina this time too, though. Like a light switch had been flicked on. She was now talking about pursuing a course in tourism.

Ella felt so proud of her she could burst. It wasn't the easiest thing going back to college after so many years and with a young son in tow.

She seemed to still be pining over Sam the author, though. He had been devastatingly handsome, and for a moment there Ella had wondered if there might be more in that romance than just a summer fling.

But clearly it wasn't to be. Such a shame.

Really that girl deserved everything. She hoped that Nina would be lucky like she herself had been, first with Gregory and now with Joseph, and find someone to love and to grow old with.

There really was no greater comfort in life.

44

Three weeks later, Nina walked from the bus stop, enjoying being outside in the cold air after being cooped up in a lecture hall all morning.

Grey clouds covered the skies and the air was chilly.

The few leaves still on the trees were golden and brown but Nina knew that in a couple of weeks, none of them would remain, and the trees would stand empty and lifeless.

Her shoes made crunching noises as she stepped on the leaves covering the path.

She thought again of Sam and wished that he could see autumn in Lakeview.

In the ensuing weeks since his departure, that

empty feeling had gone, and in its place a sadness that followed her wherever she was.

He never completely left her mind though. He appeared when she least expected, the image of his face swimming before her eyes, so close if she reached out she could touch him.

Those were the times when she missed him with a longing that bordered on being physically painful. She often wondered what he was doing, but knowing nothing of his life, it was difficult to imagine.

So she conjured up a picture of how he had described his house and his everyday routine. Her favourite image was one of him in faded jeans, sprawled out in his back garden or on the sofa, reading a book, his eyebrows creased in concentration.

Deliberately she yanked her mind away from Sam. Thoughts of him always left her low and demotivated.

Instead, she thought about her new classes in tourism. Nina enjoyed her lectures, but it still felt good when Friday came.

It was her time to relax and be with her son. She rarely worked in the cafe once the summer rush was over, and her weekends now consisted of walks with Patrick, dinner at her dad's house, and homework.

Patrick found it hilarious that his mother had homework too.

She neared the entrance door of her flat and when she looked up; Nina thought she could see the outline of a man standing on the steps of the building.

She quickened her pace, trying to make out who it was. Her dad maybe? But no he had a key ....

As the outline became clearer, Nina stared ahead in disbelief. Could it be?

It *was* ...

Sam stood up when he saw her, and walked to meet her. Without thinking, Nina dropped her bag and ran into his arms.

She drank in the masculine scent of him, forgetting to compose herself. She wanted to cry and laugh at the same time.

Then she stepped back and looked at him in disbelief.

"It's really you."

Sam laughed. "It's such a treat to see you. For the last few weeks I kept imagining how it would feel to see you and to hold you, but nothing came close to how I feel just now."

"How do you feel?" she gasped.

Sam's chest visibly rose as he inhaled deeply. "As if I've come home."

Nina fell into his arms again and then led him

inside. She pulled him into the hallway, not caring who saw her, and shut the door.

Upstairs in her flat, they turned to each other and kissed hungrily.

She felt herself melting into him. He ran his hands over her back and pulled her close. "How long till Patrick ...?" he began.

"An hour," she breathed.

"That's just about enough time for what I have in mind. God, I've missed you, Nina," Sam said.

How had she managed without him? she asked herself.

And how would she manage when he left yet again?

45

They hadn't spoken about anything, but now lying in his arms, even more questions swirled in her mind.

Reluctantly, Nina pushed herself up and went into the bathroom. Sam followed her and they stood together under the warm water.

By the time they came out of the shower, there was no time left to talk, and they dressed hurriedly.

The school bus stopped in front of the flat the moment Sam and Nina reached the living room.

"Good timing eh?" she smiled.

"If it were up to you, we would still be upstairs."

"True." She took a step back and watched as Sam exchanged high fives with Patrick. She loved that he got on so well with her son.

Nina couldn't take her eyes off Sam as later the three of them sat together and ate. He was even more handsome than she remembered.

"So did your publishers like your book?" Patrick asked.

Sam grinned. "They did. That's why I haven't been in touch, and I apologise. There was a lot more editing than I'd hoped, and I've been pretty much under lock and key for the last few weeks trying to get it ready for production. But it's done now and I'm on a roll actually," he said. "Ready to start my next one. That's why I'm back. I'd going to stay for a couple of months this time."

"Oh," Nina said, feeling a stab of disappointment.

Of course.

A LITTLE WHILE LATER, Patrick finished his food and then went to his room.

When they were once again alone, Sam leaned forward and whispered. "I lied."

"What?" Nina said distractedly.

"I came back because I can't spend one more day without you. I love you, Nina."

Her heart swelled until she thought it would burst from her chest. He *loved* her?

"I just want us to get to know each other more, spend some proper time together - all three of us - and see where it goes. How does that sound?"

It sounded perfect to Nina, and she said so. "But what about your work?" she asked.

He shrugged. "I'm a writer, I can work from anywhere."

They sat quietly contemplating each other. Nina was not a great believer in miracles but sitting there with Sam, it felt like one had just happened.

"Tell me about the tourism course," he said chatting easily, and Nina embarked on a description of her lecturers and fellow students, making him laugh with her comical portrayals.

And much later that night, when Patrick had gone to bed and Sam had retired to his newly rented cottage, Nina went to bed content just knowing that he was here in Lakeview, just a stone's throw away.

THEY VERY QUICKLY FELL INTO the routine they had before Sam left.

One day, the three of them went for a walk on the trail, enjoying it for a few more weeks before it got too boggy and the rain made it impassable.

"You'll get to see winter here after all," Nina said to him.

"Don't you know that's the main reason I came back," he teased.

The meadow was quiet, the butterflies had long returned to their hiding places.

Still she liked the silence that covered the trail now. There were no voices of people, just the swish of the wind as it went past the trees and the grass.

She smiled and took Sam's hand, as Patrick raced ahead of them.

Those glorious days of summer might have ended for everyone else, but for Nina, they would continue for a long time to come.

ABOUT THE AUTHOR

International #1 and USA Today bestselling author Melissa Hill lives in County Wicklow, Ireland.

Her page-turning emotional stories of family, friendship and romance have been translated into 25 different languages and are regular chart-toppers internationally.

A Reese Witherspoon x Hello Sunshine adaptation of her worldwide bestseller SOMETHING FROM TIFFANY'S is airing now on Amazon Prime Video worldwide.

THE CHARM BRACELET aired in 2020 as a holiday movie 'A Little Christmas Charm'. A GIFT TO REMEMBER (and a sequel) was also adapted for screen by Crown Media and multiple other titles by Melissa are currently in development for film and TV.

www.melissahill.info

Printed in Great Britain
by Amazon